W9-BFT-894

PEARLS FOR A KING

PEARLS FOR A KING

Six Short Stories Inspired by Bible Characters

Dorothy Hoyer Scharlemann

Publishing House
St. Louis

Concordia Publishing House, St. Louis, Missouri

MANUFACTURED IN THE UNITED STATES OF AMERICA

Library of Congress Cataloging in Publication Data

Scharlemann, Dorothy Hoyer, 1912-
Pearls for a King, and other stories.

CONTENTS: Aryth.—Breakfast for Matthias.—Tabita.
[etc.]
I. Title.
PZ3.S2983Pe [PS3569.C474] 813'.5'4 76-4101
ISBN 0-570-03260-1

To Martin and John
who fill my life
with love and laughter.

Contents

Adam 11
Tabitha 31
Pearls for a King 65
Breakfast for Matthias 85
Aryth 95
Joel of Tarsus 119

PEARLS FOR A KING

Adam

He leaned lightly on his hoe, and the jacaranda blossoms drifted like perfumed butterflies about him, falling in a soft purple blanket on the upturned, red-brown soil. He was proud of that hoe. By fastening the chipped stone to the end of a straight, sturdy stick he had fashioned an instrument that enabled him to turn over twice as much soil in half the time, and with far less fatigue. He bent his powerful muscles to the work, smiling with satisfaction, and wondered why he had not thought of it sooner.

A shadow dimmed for a moment the brightness of his eye. *Had* he thought of it himself, or had he been told? There had been a time when he knew, when the Voice had spoken to him clearly and with certainty. In every phase of their new life they had been given explicit instructions for each new problem as it arose. Now he could no longer be sure. Was it his own idea, this hoe? It did not really matter, he supposed. Yet it troubled him not to know. And it troubled him even more when he realized that, much as he yearned to hear the Voice again, some of his sense of satisfaction faded when he realized the idea might not have been his own.

What did it matter? The radiant love that had spoken through the Voice surrounded him still. The sunshine, the vibrantly glowing reds and yellows and oranges of the blossoming trees and hedges, the lush green of the meadow grasses, the two sturdy boys working in the fields, the girl laughing in the cave with her mother, the blue sky above and the dark clouds forming in the west that promised the life-giving rain—all was good, in spite of the struggle and the pain that had invaded their lives. There had been a time, but he could remember it only vaguely.

He took a deep breath and straightened his broad shoulders. Now, if he could somehow manage to fasten this instrument he called a hoe to the horse and teach him to pull it while he himself weighted it and drove it into the ground, that would surely lighten his work further.

A shout exploded the sunlit silence about him. He began to laugh. In a nearby field Cain had already done it. He was driving one of the smallest of the horses before him, tied with leather thongs to the sharp stick he had been using, plowing an uncertain row across the sun-warmed earth. It tore up the surface weeds and turned over the damp red soil, softening and loosening it, opening it up to the seed they would sow on the morrow. Had the Voice spoken to Cain? Or was there something within a man that gave him power and knowledge to work out his own solutions to the problems life now set before him?

He shouted back and waved a congratulatory arm to the excited boy. He had thought of it, too, but Cain had turned it into action, and he would be given all credit for the discovery. It pleased him that Cain was sharp-witted and practical. As he grew older he would be a tremendous help in the daily struggle for food that life had become.

It had not always been so. He could remember—he thought he could remember—it had all become vague and indistinct. Except the Voice. That memory was sharp within him. It had once spoken clearly—so clearly there could be no mistaking it—but it had spoken only of love and companionship. There had been no need for instruction or explanation, only the one caution. And the shadow returned to his eyes, and the dread blackness over his soul as he thrust with his hoe into the slowly yielding soil. Ah, if only the Voice would speak again, clearly and lovingly! Yet it was surely a gift from him who had spoken that had enabled Adam to think of the hoe and Cain of the plow.

Eve had never spoken of the Voice. Yet she had known instinctively what to do when the children had been born. And he winced at the memory of the pain she had endured. There was nothing vague or indistinct about that memory. Yet she had borne no ill will against the cause of her suffering, accepting each child as a gift from the Lord, nourishing and loving it with a tender care that sometimes brought tears to his eyes. Once there had been no tears either. Would there ever be a time again when there would be no tears, and the Voice would speak plainly and in love?

With an exclamation he dashed the sweat from his brow and bent his back to the hoe. The earth must be turned and the seed sown if they were to eat when the world turned cold and the earth no longer gave of its fruits. Later he would examine Cain's new invention and try it out himself.

A scream startled him. It was Abel among his sheep. Adam dropped his hoe and ran. The boy was laying about him with a stout stick, and a snarl and sharp howl indicated that he was doing it most effectively. A long grey shadow streaked off into the woods, but Abel dropped to his knees, and when Adam reached him he was sobbing piteously over the torn and bleeding body of the lamb he held in his arms. Adam knelt beside him. The lamb bleated softly, struggled a moment, and then lay still. Adam put his arms around the sobbing boy.

"It is death," he said, and he wondered how he knew. "It will not live again." He thought of the Voice, and this time the memory was sharp and clear: "You are dust, and to dust you shall return."

"We must return it to the earth," said Adam gently. "Otherwise the animals will come again to devour it." He had once had power over the animals; he had called them by their name. No more. Except for a few—the horse that cropped the grasses close by the cave and bore their burdens, the dog, the cow, the sheep, a few others—the animals were alien to him now. They lived in the forest, and by night he could hear their growlings and their howlings. But this was the first time one had come near enough to attack the sheep.

Adam shivered, and a new dread wrapped itself around him. Would there be worse horrors before deliverance came, before the seed of the woman would crush the head of evil? Again he remembered his bewilderment when Eve bore not the one child who was to crush evil and bring their deliverance, but in the course of time, three tiny babes, two in his form and one in hers, all weaker and more helpless than any lamb or foal the animals around them had produced. They were growing to sturdy manhood and womanhood now, these children, but which was to be their deliverer?

The eldest, surely. But Cain had come running, and Adam felt a sharp revulsion at the look of fascinated horror on the boy's face as he bent over the torn lamb in his brother's arms.

Abel's sobs had quieted somewhat. Adam took the lamb gently from his arms, and with sharp sticks they dug a hole and placed the stiffening body inside, covering it gently with the loose earth. This, then, was what the Voice meant by "to dust you shall return." Would he himself be returned to the dust before deliverance came? Surely, before then Cain would have fashioned deliverance for them all. Yet the Voice had spoken directly to him—"to dust you shall return"—and there was no avoiding that sentence. It seemed to him a thing more sharply to be dreaded than anything he had yet experienced, and he could not bear even to think of it.

A clear call came from the direction of the cave. He raised Abel to his feet.

"Tomorrow," he said gently, "we will build a wall—something to enfold the sheep and keep them safe. Now the sun is setting, and it is time to eat and rest. Let us go home."

The boys ran ahead of him toward the cave, through the flaming sunset that never ceased to remind him with pain of the cherubim and the flaming sword that cut him off from . . . What was it that he only dimly remembered?

Harvests followed seedtime, cold followed heat, night

followed day and day night, in a rhythm that never varied. Cain, grown almost as tall as his father and fully as handsome—though there was a flaw about his eyes that troubled Adam—had found the cave too confining for his restless spirit and had set up his own shelter of animal skins some distance off. Abel—tall and strong, but with an openness about his face that Cain somehow lacked—had built a shelter near the sheepfold where he could more easily guard his flock. Zilphah, with her mother's gracious loveliness disguising a sometimes wayward will of her own, remained with her parents in the cave. But she was often with her brothers, helping Abel at lambing time and with the shearing, or gathering with Cain the harvests of his fields. Hers was an outdoor spirit that cared little for the preparing of meals or the combing and cleaning of the fibers of wool that Eve had so cleverly learned to twist and weave into cloth.

It troubled Adam that the Voice had not spoken for so long. The children were growing into adulthood without having heard it—perhaps without even realizing that there existed a Presence beyond their own to which they owed allegiance. They knew of the Promise, of course. He had seen to that. But they knew it only as an abstract future in which they would be delivered from all the evils and difficulties that annoyed them. Of the past and why the Promise was so sure, how much did they really comprehend?

Suddenly he realized that the fault was his. From their childhood on he should have been telling them of whatever memories remained to him. Perhaps the telling itself might have firmed the shifting outlines of his memory so that he would have known more surely what had happened in the beginning. But he had been so busy!

Under the stars, where the evening fire was always lit when the weather was fair, Adam gathered his family about him and began to speak to them of what had been. And as he spoke, he could not be sure whether it was memory that gave his words meaning or something outside himself that prompted his speech.

"In the beginning," he said slowly, "God created the world. It was shapeless and empty, covered with water and shrouded in darkness. But the Spirit of God brooded over the face of the waters, and God said: 'Let there be light!' And there was light. And God loved the light and separated it from the darkness."

Abel listened raptly, but Cain with an amused indifference that irritated Adam. Zilphah, too, was more prone to giggle at Cain's sidelong glances and surreptitious teasings than to listen to her father's solemn voice.

Watching them as he spoke, the slow realization came to Adam that his children were no longer children. The urge to love was growing strong in them, as it was in himself when he looked across the fire at Eve's glowing loveliness. A sudden apprehension seized him. If ever he needed the Voice to tell him what to do, it was now. He broke off his narrative abruptly.

"Cain," he said severely, "have you ever thought what it means that you are alive?"

Cain stared.

"You will have no understanding of life and of its meaning unless you know and understand the meaning of what I am trying to tell you. I expect you to listen with attention and intelligence."

"Ah, well," Cain stretched his long legs toward the fire. "All that about the Voice and the Garden, it is just a myth, you know. Things have always been as they are now, and they always will be."

"Besides," said Zilphah pertly, "Mother has told us all those stories ever since we were tiny babies!"

Adam's jaw dropped in astonishment. Abel laughed.

"Never mind, Father," he said. "There is somehow a greater meaning when you tell of it."

"Yes," smiled Eve. "I spoke as to children, and to them they were only lovely stories. But you are right. Now they must understand them as men and women, to know the meaning and the pain." Her clear voice lingered into silence as it did so often when memory overcame her.

But Cain would have no more of it. He rose and stretched his arms above his head. "I must be up with the dawn," he said. "The corn is nearly ripe, and the tools must be prepared for the harvesting. Zilphah," he added carelessly, "I am hungry. Will you bring some of that delicious honey we found yesterday to my tent?"

Eve looked up sharply, and Adam noticed the shadow of concern that crossed her face. They were never far apart in their awareness, and he wondered if she knew now what must be done. But Abel had sprung to his feet.

"She shall not go with you to your tent!" He almost spat it out, and there was a darkening of suspicious anger on his usually sunny face. Bewildered, Zilphah looked from one to the other of her handsome brothers, and Adam noted the look of dawning excitement in her face.

"Zilphah," said Eve smoothly, "get a little honey for Cain, but he shall carry it to his tent himself. You will remain here with us."

Obediently, Zilphah rose, and from the little storage shelf in a niche in the cave scraped a little of the waxy sweet into a palm leaf and brought it to Cain. He nodded his thanks, touched her cheek gently with his powerful fingers, and with a glance of frustrated hostility at his brother, disappeared into the night. Abel, his face slightly puzzled but still dark with anger, strode off toward his sheepfold, while Zilphah, uneasy at the tension she felt she had caused but could not understand, withdrew into the farthest reaches of the cave to her bed of fragrant pine boughs, covered with the soft matted fleece of sheep's wool—a gift from Abel.

Not a word had been spoken, and the two parents continued to sit in silence across the fire from each other. They had no need of speech. After a while Eve rose and came to him, pressed her cheek to his soft beard, drew her hand in a gentle caress across his shoulders, and left him. The responsibility was his.

He threw a few more sticks on the fire and watched as the flames darted up toward the starry sky. His problems surrounded him like the forces of evil itself. He was beginning to suspect that the real evil in his broken world lay not so much in the wild animals of the forest, or the untimely rains that could ruin the harvest, nor even in the constant struggle against drought and weed and insect, but within man himself. How far those terrible glances between his two sons had fallen from the image of God in which he himself had been created!

How could it have happened that the Voice, the Presence of the Lord God himself, after which he yearned with the whole strength and sensitivity of his being, could have become for his children merely pleasant tales with which to lull a child to sleep? Certainly he could not blame Eve. She had done better than he.

He had not intended it to be so. He had simply not foreseen. He had hugged to himself the pain of his fading memories, when he should have shared them with his children, pain and all, in order that they might understand.

Nor was it only pain. Not a day passed that he did not take joy in the solid green earth beneath his feet, in the strength of his own body, in the sun, the rain, the sparkling depth of the night sky with its changeable moon, as delicate as Eve herself. His blessings had always exceeded his problems, and his gratitude toward the love that bestowed them on him had been a healing balm to his pain.

But his children knew neither pain nor blessing. He thought of Cain's careless words: "Things have always been as they are now, and always will be." How could he make them understand their blessings? How could they learn to acknowledge that all good came from the love behind the Voice they regarded as merely a "myth"? How could they experience the joy of gratitude? They knew gratitude among themselves. Cain had thanked Zilphah in his own way for serving him. How could he, their father, after all this time, instill in them love and gratitude towards their God and Maker?

And now a new problem had arisen—the rivalry of the two young men and the vulnerability of his daughter. His blessings surely exceeded his problems, but the problems required a solution, and he felt with a sort of panic that disaster lay within this one.

But first, surely, must come an acknowledgment of the sovereignty of the Voice of the Lord God, an expression of gratitude for his love and adoration of his greatness. He thrust more wood onto the fire and watched as the sparks flew up and mingled their golden glitter with the silver of the stars. The fire! What better way than to return to the Lord of their blessings—by fire? The leaping warmth and light that flamed in answer to the heat and light of the sun, that greatest of his blessings!

Excited, he rose to his feet. In the morning they would build platforms—altars—on which each of his sons would offer a little of the best of their blessings as a sign that all belonged to the Lord God and that their hearts turned to him in gratitude. How could they fail to understand?

Abel was enthusiastic about the plan and began eagerly assembling heavy flat stones for his altar. Cain shrugged his broad shoulders but, obedient as always, followed suit. Yet Adam had the feeling that it was only because Abel's altar took shape so rapidly and so skillfully that Cain put any effort at all into his work. Here, of course, Abel had the advantage. He had worked with stones for years, enlarging his sheepfold as the flock grew, and building himself a shelter. Adam could sense Cain's frustration as the stones would not fit or would balance only precariously, and once even fell and would surely have crushed his bare foot had he not been agile enough to spring lightly aside.

Finally the two altars stood finished. In the morning, at sunrise, the family would gather before the altars. Cain would bring the first fruits of his harvest—the first cuttings of the fully ripened grain. Abel would bring his—a newborn lamb. And it was the thought of this newborn lamb that gave Adam some sleepless hours that night.

There was no doubt that Cain's offering, the dry stalks of golden ripe wheat, would burn. The flame and smoke would rise easily to the heavens, above which dwelt the God who had created them. But the lamb? And what would be the effect on Abel's enthusiasm should his offering not burn?

Adam tossed uneasily on his mat. The whole idea was a wretched mistake. And it had been so well-intentioned and seemed so logical. Yet his good intentions so often went wrong!

Perhaps it did not really matter. Both boys had known from early childhood that it was Cain, the eldest, the "man from the Lord," as Eve had called him, who was to be their deliverer. Abel had always accepted it without question, even into young manhood, even when Cain had taunted him with the fact of the Promise.

Perhaps that had been another mistake. Perhaps Cain should not have been made so early aware of his superior position. It came to Adam with a shock that the Promise had filled Cain with an arrogance that had not been intended by Adam nor surely by the Voice. There it was again. How was it that everything he planned, everything that at its inception seemed good and right and pleasing to the Lord, should at its fruition lie twisted and broken at his feet, as if some malicious, alien power were bent on his destruction, on that of his family, and on all humankind? Was it possible that not only he, but his children and his children's children were to suffer forever under the curse he and Eve had brought upon themselves by their pride and disobedience?

Not forever. The Promise was there. The woman's seed should crush the serpent's head. Their offspring would deliver them from the evil that threatened at every turn. How Cain should accomplish this would undoubtedly become clear at the proper time. They must wait for their deliverance, but the waiting already seemed so long!

But for tomorrow, should the fire be unable to consume Abel's newborn lamb, should Abel feel that his offering was rejected by the Lord, he would have to present the same, somewhat worn explanation: Cain was the elder, chosen by the Lord to be their deliverer, and this was the way the choice was made yet clearer. It seemed a most inadequate explanation, but it was the best Adam could think of at the moment, and he finally fell asleep.

Abel prepared his offering with great care. He had long ago lost his horror over the death of any of his sheep. He had too often been faced with the problem of an injured or sick and dying animal, and it had come to him that it was more merciful to kill the animal with a quick slash of the throat than to allow it to linger in its suffering.

But for the Lord there would be no injured or sick lamb. This must be one without blemish and without spot—the most perfect of the firstlings of his flock. In the predawn hours he killed and dressed it. He laid the wood with great care: first the dried leaves and twigs that would catch the spark of flint, then the larger branches of dead wood that were to be found wherever there were trees, and finally larger logs, old and well dried, that would keep the fire at a steady flame until the lamb had been consumed.

Cain was not so careful about his offering. He had no need to be. More than once he had been made painfully aware of the power of fire over his fields of ripening grain. A few leaves and twigs, a little wood—the grain itself would burn as well.

But Cain was annoyed, nevertheless. A whole day had been wasted building those ridiculous piles of stone at his father's whim. It had, of course, never occurred to him to disobey, but someday soon he was going to cut loose from his father's dominance and choose fields to plow a great way off, so that he could do things in his own way and at times of his own choosing. Even now he ought to be in the field, cutting great swaths of the golden grain with his powerful arms, rejoicing in the strength and precision with which he layered the rows, ready for gathering. Instead he cut a meager handful and brought it to lay upon his altar.

Both young men knelt as they struck their flints together to produce the sparks that would ignite the fires. To Adam and Eve and Zilphah, watching nearby, it seemed good to kneel, too, in the freshness of the morning dew, in adoration of the Lord in whose honor the offerings were being given. As the red-gold sun appeared over the low hills to the east, the dry twigs and leaves began to crackle with flame, and Adam felt a rising sense of satisfaction within him. It was good to give thanks to the Lord, to present to him in gratitude these tokens of his blessings. Surely, his sons must feel that as well as he. He bowed his head in adoration.

A gust of wind.

It could have been nothing more. It snuffed out Cain's fire before the sacrificial grain had even been scorched. Aghast, Adam sprang to his feet.

"We will relight it," he said, reaching for Cain's flint. But Cain struck his hand aside.

"Let it be," he said angrily. "If your Lord will not accept my offering, neither will I have anything more to do with him!" He rose to his feet and stalked angrily off to his tent.

Uncertain, Adam stared after him. He would have followed, but Abel's offering must not be neglected. Already the odor of singed wool and roasting flesh rose with the smoke up to the clouding heavens. What did it mean? What could it mean but that Abel was the chosen of the Lord, the deliverer? And to Adam it seemed that his younger son's head was bowed not so much in adoration as in an attempt to hide the triumph that must show on his open face. Adam groaned within himself as he fell once more to his knees. The pride that had been his own downfall lived on in his sons as well. He could not escape it. Again he felt that sense of impending disaster and the agonizing knowledge that he could do nothing to prevent it.

When the lamb had at last been consumed, Adam rose heavily to his feet. He laid his hand on the still-bent head of his son and said: "The Lord bless you, Abel!" He turned to meet Eve's troubled eyes, nodded, and said: "I will speak to Cain." As he turned toward the tent, he glimpsed Zilphah rising to her feet to greet Abel with her most enchanting smile.

He found Cain almost cowering in a corner of his tent, white and shaken.

"The Voice!" he said hoarsely. "Your Voice has spoken to me!"

Adam's heart gave a great leap. All would yet be well if the Voice had returned. He waited.

"It said if I did well, should I not be accepted?" His voice had lost it's quiver, and he rose angrily to his feet. With human contact his bravado seemed to be returning. "How have I not done well? I have done what you asked and offered to the Lord as you told me to offer. How does Abel do well and not I?"

Still Adam waited, despair rising within him.

"'Sin lies at the door,' it said. What sin? Wherein have I sinned? I have offered to the Lord exactly as Abel has. Why does sin wait for me and not for Abel?"

"Sin is of the heart," said Adam heavily, "not only in the act."

"You have lied to me about the Voice!" Cain turned on him savagely. "You spoke of love and blessing in the Voice. To me it speaks of sin and warns of judgment. Those are not the words of a God of love!"

"But there is love in warning!" cried Adam, stung at last to defense. But in his heart he thought: I have failed again. Only too well he knew how the Voice could speak in judgment, yet he had not told his children of it. Neither, he supposed, had Eve. They had been concerned only that the children should know the Lord God by his love. Or was it, again, only their pride that had kept them from speaking of his judgment?

"I go to speak with Abel," said Cain, brushing rudely past his father and out of the tent. Every instinct within Adam cried out that Cain must be stopped; yet he did nothing. Despairingly he admitted that his children had grown beyond him and must take responsibility for their own actions.

Sick at heart, Adam left the tent and returned to the two altars, Abel's still warm and glowing, Cain's cold, its offering lying untouched. In wild anger at his own impotence, Adam gathered up the wilting stalks and dashed them to the ground. It had been a stupid idea. No—he would not so deny his own intentions. It had been a good and noble thought. But, again, it had been distorted by the evil that continually surrounded and frustrated him, and which he was beginning to think of as a powerful force against which he could not contend. Not alone. There must come a deliverer. The Promise was there; it stood firm. But who was the deliverer, now, and when would deliverance come?

In the distance he saw the two young men walking together toward Cain's golden field. In spite of his apprehension he could not help rejoicing in the strength of their lithe young bodies and the grace of their movements. Ah, well, he thought, they are brothers, and their love for each other will overcome Cain's anger and hurt. All will yet be well. He turned toward the cave to gather up his tools for the day's work.

He felt the cry before he heard it. Whirling, he saw Cain alone in the field, bending over some dreadful thing on the ground beside him. He raced toward his son, ran as he had never run before, yet, as in a nightmare, never seemed to come nearer the kneeling figure. Cain saw him coming, sprang to his feet, and disappeared into the neighboring woods.

Adam lifted the waxen face and bloodied head into his arms, but knew he was too late. He remembered the time Abel had knelt so, the dead and torn lamb in his arms—their first experience of violent death—and a great sob broke in his throat. It suddenly released a tightness within him that had been long building, but left in its place a bleak despair such as he had never known, not even on that black day when they had been forced to leave the Garden. Now all was lost—the Promise, their hope of a deliverer. Cain had destroyed it all, as surely as he and Eve had destroyed the Paradise they had expected Cain to restore to them. He bent his head over his dead son and sobbed, but was afforded no release.

After a while it came to him with a dim sort of conviction that he must find Cain. If there was to be any future for them at all, no matter how twisted or broken, Cain must be found. He laid the battered head gently on the ground, rose stiffly to his feet, and blindly, without any sense of direction, made for the woods where he had seen Cain disappear.

He searched for a long time among the great trees, past fallen giants that had been split and broken by lightning, through tangled vines and thorny briers that hindered him at every step. After a while he began to call, softly at first, then more and more loudly as his anxiety grew. He was positive that Cain heard him;

yet there was no answer. His voice sharpened in anger as he stumbled ever deeper into the gloom of the forest. How could the boy have so ruined himself and destroyed all their hopes because of a wind-extinguished fire?

"Cain!"

The forest birds hushed their song and the squirrels their chatter at the roar of his voice, but the only reply was the low rumble of thunder from the coming storm. He glanced up. Through a clearing in the towering branches he glimpsed the darkening clouds and knew he must turn back. He could not deliberately endanger his life in a violent storm here in the forest. There were two women dependent on him—now on him alone.

"Cain!"

His fury grew as he made his way back toward the clearing and the cave. Cain, after all, might not have penetrated so far into the forest. Yet why did he not respond?

"Cain!"

He paused, breathing heavily. The silence around him was ominous and threatening. In a sudden flash he remembered another call, in a Garden vastly different from this, and in a Voice that held no anger, only sorrow and a great love: "Adam, where are you?" In desperation he let out one more call, hearing it fall flat and dead against the humid, stifling air. But again, no answer.

He had done all he could. He must return to Abel before the dark and the storm and the marauding animals. Then it came to him with a sense of shock that Abel was no longer there. That bright and laughing spirit, with the open, sunny smile—where had it gone? Did it wander in some shadowy and featureless world, alone, unhappy? The broken and lifeless body must be returned to the earth: "You are dust, and to dust you shall return." But the thing that had given life to the body, that had taught it thought and speech and laughter . . . It was inconceivable that it could vanish into nothingness. He would never know, of course, until he himself came to that end. But as he emerged from the woods, he felt with a conviction born of memory that the Lord God who had in love given life to the body, would in love preserve that life and take it back to himself.

He found Eve deathly white and still, holding the battered head in her lap, and Zilphah kneeling beside her, sobbing wildly. In spite of the gathering storm, he took the time to dig deep into the earth for safety against the wild animals. Eve brought water and washed the handsome, waxen face and body, while Zilphah brought the soft fleece that had been Abel's gift to her. They wrapped him in it gently, then returned him to the earth, to which they would all in time return. They knew it now; for them there was no escape: "You are dust, and to dust you shall return."

The storm broke just as they reached the cave and, because they had made no preparation, almost immediately washed out their fire. Adam patiently went about kindling a new flame deeper under the shelter of the rock, while Eve set food before them, but no one had the heart to eat. They did not brood long over the fire that night, but soon sought their beds, each in loneliness and heartbreak.

Only Zilphah slept, and that fitfully. Over the thresh of the rain Adam could hear the occasional deep sobs that broke into her disturbed rest. Eve lay motionless, eyes wide and tearless in the firelit dark. With each flash of lightning and crash of thunder she seemed to shrink further into herself, and Adam wished that she would cry. He laid his hand gently on her shoulder, but she did not respond. He longed to comfort her, but could find no words.

He thought of his two sons and knew that she thought of them also. Of Abel, gone forever, his place marked only by the little mound from which the pouring rain would long since have washed away the flowers they had heaped upon it.

He thought of Cain, wandering in the rain through the dark and evil forest. Were his thoughts as dark and evil? Or might it be remorse and despair that drove him on? Again Adam felt the sharp ache of his own ineptitude. He had sought Cain in anger and in selfish concern over his own future. The Promise? After all, it was the Lord God who had made the Promise, and it stood firm. It was not Adam's responsibility to see that it was fulfilled.

Had he shown Cain the same love and sorrow the Voice had once shown them in the Garden—had he shown concern for his son rather than terror at his own broken future—perhaps Cain would have responded.

But surely Cain would return. He would not so abandon the ripening fields he loved, the tent that sheltered him, the family that had nurtured him. Even now he was undoubtedly back in his tent, seeking shelter from the rain. Tomorrow, he, Adam, would show his son, Cain, that a father's love could forgive and restore, just as forgiveness and restoration awaited them all with the coming of the promised deliverer—whoever that might now be, and whenever the Lord God chose to send him.

With the dawn, Adam arose. Eve had finally dropped into a restless slumber, and he slipped out of the cave as noiselessly as he could. The long grasses were wet and chill, but the air was fresh and clear. A new day. Would the Lord God continue his blessings? Oh, that he would show them the way to a new life, one not flawed by their own faults and inadequacies! Hope came with activity, and he was not surprised to see Cain sitting before the entrance to his tent.

But how different! His arms rested on his knees, his hands dangling loosely before him. His bowed back and drooping head spoke eloquently of the despair in his heart. Yet, as Adam approached, the head suddenly lifted in the old arrogant defiance, and Adam heard him say: "I do not know; am I my brother's keeper?"

Adam stopped short, but Cain was not speaking to him. He listened intently, yet he could hear nothing. Cain also listened, and Cain heard. The defiance in his face changed to sudden horror. He sprang to his feet in protest, one arm raised as if to ward off a blow. Then the arm sank; the head bowed; the knees gave way, and he crumpled to the ground and stretched himself prone upon his face.

Appalled, Adam shrank back. Had the Lord God forgotten his mercy? Would the Voice pronounce judgment and slay in the same breath? But he heard Cain moan, and the words came out in great gasps of pain:

"My punishment is great, greater than I can bear! You are driving me away from the ground, from everything I love. Even from your face I will be hidden! A fugitive and a wanderer, and everyone that sees me will try to kill me!"

Sobs began to tear through his body, but stopped almost immediately as he lifted his head to listen. Then the head sank low again into the wet grass. For a moment he lay still; then a sudden convulsive shock almost lifted the great body from the ground. He threw out his arms, wrenched himself around upon his back, and again lay quite still.

So long did he lie motionless that Adam thought: The Voice has surely killed him. With a great yearning he thought: My son! Yet perhaps it was better so. As a fugitive and wanderer, he would never feel contentment again.

Trembling, he approached his son and knelt to touch him. With one lithe, powerful movement Cain sprang to his feet, towering over his still kneeling father. Adam had not felt fear since the time he had hidden in the Garden, yet now he shrank back in terror at the blazing power on the face of his son.

"What is it?" Cain passed his hand over his face. "The Voice has put his mark on me that none should kill me. Am I hideous?"

"No, no!" Adam took a deep breath and rose to his feet. "There is no disfigurement. Only, such a look will bring fear. None will dare to stand against you!"

"Ah!" Cain's sigh was almost a shudder. "So I must go alone. All men will fear me, and I must wander alone. Even the ground has cursed me because it has drunk my brother's blood. Look!"

With a cry that froze Adam's heart he stretched his arm toward the fields he was to have harvested that day. It took an enormous effort to follow Cain's pointing. The grain that had so proudly waved its golden heads in yesterday's sunshine lay flat and sodden and lifeless on the ground. Cain dropped to his knees, hid his face in his hands, and began to sob like a child, while Adam stood helplessly by.

After a while they went together toward the cave. It seemed the only logical thing to do. Adam thought with apprehension, What will he do when he sees the look of fear on the faces of Eve and Zilphah, when they shrink before him as I did just now?

There was no fear, only sorrow and a great love. Adam thought: Their gentle spirits have never been a threat to Cain, nor have their lesser strengths. So then why should they now know fear? It was as it should be; yet he had not expected it.

White-faced, yet with great practicality, Eve went about gathering such food and necessities as she could find to speed Cain on his endless journey. He accepted the gifts from her humbly and gratefully. Wordlessly he embraced them all, knelt at Adam's feet for his blessing, and turned to go.

He had taken only a few steps when an echo stirred in Adam's thoughts. "Wait!" he called. He reached down and took Zilphah's hand. She looked up, smiling assent through her tears. Together they approached Cain.

"It is not good that man should be alone," said Adam, and placed Zilphah's hand into Cain's. Without a word or backward glance, they walked together toward the little hillock that finally hid them from view.

Adam dared not turn around. His heart beat wildly. Had he done wisely? Or was this another of his well-intentioned but colossal mistakes? He had robbed Eve of the last of her children, and what must she feel now?

He felt her presence beside him. She looked up into his agonized eyes with a half-smile and a slight nod of consent.

Then suddenly her white face twisted, she closed her eyes, and the tears began to pour down her cheeks. He took her in his arms and held her close, while the mother of all living mourned the loss of her children.

There is a bit of Paradise left to us yet, thought Adam, as he checked the horse and leaned lightly on his plow. Eve was kneeling by the water's edge, filling the half shell of a large gourd he had scooped out and dried for her. The boy was lying on his stomach, paddling in the water with his tiny hands. As she set the gourd carefully upon the ground, the boy kicked at it with his feet, upsetting the gourd and propelling himself with a splash into the water. In one quick sweep Eve drew him out of the stream, overturned him on her knees, and smartly spanked his round little bottom. The boy howled and struggled, and Adam smiled to himself. Seth is just like the rest of us, he thought, with a will and a pride of his own. He had long ago dismissed from his thoughts the expectation that a natural child of his own might be their deliverer. It would take some powerful intervention on the part of the Lord God himself to bring to birth one who would live in the perfect obedience he himself had failed to achieve. But he never doubted the Promise. The Promise held firm. Some day the Voice that he had not heard since they left the Garden would speak again, the forces of evil that surrounded them would be crushed and thoroughly broken by the Deliverer, and the Garden would be open to them again.

Meanwhile he spoke to the horse and leaned his massive strength against the plow as the earth unfolded in a long, rich furrow beneath his feet. Eve and Seth, friends again, were climbing hand in hand up the path to the cave. Yes, thought Adam, no matter how many generations pass before deliverance comes, there is a bit of Paradise left to us still.

(This story is based on the Biblical account given in Genesis 3:23 to 4:17a.)

Tabitha

Tabitha looked up, startled. Above the grinding of her millstone she had heard strange noises—shouts and a queer, chopping, clopping noise. Almost before she could rise to her feet it was there—great pawing hooves, powerful legs, huge brown body, tossing mane, and flashing eyes—and on it a strange man in strange clothing, looking down at her with fierce blue eyes above a great black beard.

He must surely have been the biggest man in the world, and she would have turned to run, except that the sword he held high above his head was flashing bright sunlight into her eyes. Frozen between fear and awe she did not move until a scream from her mother inside the little mud-brick house and a strange, suddenly choked-off cry from her father brought her back to action. But as she turned to run, she heard the sword clanging back into the scabbard and felt herself caught up in powerful arms and deposited high up on the rearing, plunging horse. In a swirl of dust the man wrenched the powerful animal around and, with a loud shout, sent it galloping down the village street. His great hand gently but firmly covered her terrified eyes, but not before she had seen other horses and other men upon them, and her own people running in panic before them or lying strangely still in heaps beside the road. She heard the crackle of flames as they passed the barley fields outside the village. The horse settled down to a long, rhythmic stride that bore them swiftly northward. By the time her captor released Tabitha's eyes, the village that had been her home had disappeared behind a low line of hills on the horizon. She never saw it again.

She was treated kindly. How kindly she did not realize until one evening when Zobar, the fat old slave into whose charge she had been given, took her away from the bustle of the nightly setting up of camp to watch the pathetic group of captives who followed them on foot. Weary, despairing, hungry, thirsty, they seemed conscious of nothing except the necessity of putting one foot ahead of the other to avoid the whips and spears of the mounted soldiers who cruelly prodded them on, circling around them like dogs around reluctant sheep. One young woman stumbled and fell to her knees just beside her, and Tabitha recognized her. Ulia!

With a shriek, Tabitha tore her hand from that of her startled guardian and threw herself upon the young woman. But Ulia's hands were tied behind her, and she could not embrace the sobbing child. She bent her head in a frantic caress, whispering into the girl's ear.

"Tabitha! You are here! Free? Go quickly, before they hurt you!" And, indeed, the whip was already raised, and Zobar only just managed to snatch her back to safety before it fell short. There were angry words between Zobar and the wheeling guard, but by then Ulia had struggled to her feet and moved on, and the whip had not touched her. Yet Tabitha could not forget the dirty, haggard face, the unkempt hair, and the despairing eyes of her mother's younger sister, the young aunt who had once seemed to her all gaity and light and laughing enchantment.

Tabitha was not taken to visit the captives again; yet she was aware, as they passed on from camp to camp, that the group grew ever larger as they moved northward. She began to understand some of the talk of her strange-tongued captors. She soon realized that the powerful, black-bearded rider who had torn her from her loved, familiar world into this maelstrom of horses and soldiers and campfires and dust was the leader of the expedition, and that he was called Naaman. They were Syrians, working their way back to their home in Damascus, exultant at presenting to their king, Benhadad, the spoils of one of the most profitable raids in recent history.

Ages later, it seemed, Tabitha awakened one morning as usual at the first light of dawn. It was so quiet about her that for a moment she thought she lay once more on the straw pallet beside her mother in the little mud brick house that had been her home. But the sky with its fading stars was open above her, and from the distance came the sound of the movement of horses as they cropped the grass in the fields nearby. It was strange that Zobar still lay near her, sound asleep; that no fires were lit, no servants moving about them preparing the morning meal, no shouts and curses from soldiers saddling their horses and readying their weapons for the day's work. The camp was still asleep, as though at the end of its journey, with nothing left either to fear or to accomplish.

Cautiously, Tabitha sat up. There were not even guards about, except one before the entrance of Naaman's tent. Looking about her, she suddenly realized why. They were home—home to these soldiers in their faraway land. She saw, in the valley below, a vast city, buildings upon buildings, gardens and orchards and two silver-flowing rivers reflecting the brightening sky. It looked green and lovely and refreshing after the heat and the dust of the hills through which they had been traveling. And the camp was still asleep because there would be no raids today. There would be a triumphal procession, and the people who lined the streets would cheer the soldiers and gasp at the wealth of the spoils and spit on the captives.

The captives! In a sudden panic she scrambled to her feet, then checked herself. She must be very, very quiet! Cautiously she crept through the rows of sleeping servants, skirted the mass of soldiers who somehow appeared much less numerous and formidable in their sleep, and approached the restless mass of rags and dirt that she knew to be the captives. Here, indeed, there were a few guards, and from behind a convenient shrub she watched them. Those nearby were looking out over the sleeping city, their voices quiet and relaxed as they pointed out various landmarks to each other. Other guards in the distance seemed to be paying just as little attention to their charges, and Tabitha felt she ran little risk of being seen. But how would she find Ulia? They all looked so alike in their dusty rags!

Ulia, quite nearby, sat up as though someone had called her. Instantly Tabitha ran to her and was drawn quickly down to the ground beside her and covered by her tattered cloak. The movement caused no stir among the guards. The pain of aching limbs and bruised flesh, and the nightmares of remembered anguish made their charges a restless lot at best, and they noticed nothing.

After her sobs had quieted in Ulia's arms, Tabitha said, "What is going to happen, Ulia?"

"Listen carefully, Tabitha. You must go back where you were. They will sell us as slaves, but I think you will be taken into the commander's household, and I think he will treat you kindly. Otherwise you would not have been so protected. Now, go quickly before you are missed or the guards find you!"

But Tabitha clung to her, and for awhile Ulia held her close. And the question came in a whisper so faint she barely heard it.

"Mother?"

But Ulia only tightened her embrace, and Tabitha knew that was the only answer she would get.

"Now, Tabby, you must go."

Tabitha shook her head. "I will stay with you."

"Child! They beat us and starve us, and drive us on without water or rest. Look at my feet!" And she thrust two horrors of dirt and bruises and dried blood out from under her rags. "We had two children with us—from another village. You did not know them, but they are both dead. You *must* go!"

Stubbornly, Tabitha clung to her. "It is not far to the town. I can walk with you. If they beat me I will not scream. And, perhaps, if the commander knows I will not leave you, he might take us both together."

It was Ulia's turn for a deep sob. "Oh, dear God, to have a kind master!" Then she forcibly pushed the child from her. "No, Tabby! More likely you will be sold, too, for your disobedience. Go now, quickly. Ah! Here are the guards!"

They came, prodding and kicking and flicking their whips, and wherever they walked the captives stumbled dazedly to their feet. Zobar was with them, and he noticed Tabitha instantly as she and Ulia stood up. He ran to her, ponderously, chattering excitedly, and grasped her by the arm. But Tabitha clung to her aunt and would not move.

The guard knew what to do. He strode toward them and raised his arm. Ulia stiffened and Tabitha gasped as the whip curled around both their backs. But Zobar, in a perfect frenzy of chatter, turned on the guard. Repeatedly, Tabitha caught the word "Naaman" in his excited, unintelligible chatter. Dubious, fierce-eyed, the guard stood listening. Then, puzzled and slightly amused, he folded his whip under his arm and watched Zobar back away, his quivering hands palm outward, in a restraining gesture which said, as clearly as if they could understand his words: "Wait! Wait! Do nothing! I will get help!" Then he turned and waddled away as fast as his fat legs would allow toward Naaman's tent.

The rest of the camp was rousing, now, as the sun began to light up the mountains behind them. One of the servants Tabitha had often seen around the cooking fires came by, just outside the circle of captives, tossing large chunks of dry bread to those agile enough to catch them. Ulia shared hers with Tabitha, but ate so hungrily the small portion she had kept for herself that Tabitha, after two small bites, declared that she could eat no more and gave it back to Ulia. Afterwards, in groups of four or five, they were taken by the guards to a small stream, already muddy and soiled by the soldiers and horses upstream. But they all drank thirstily for the few moments they were allowed to kneel by the sullied water.

Zobar did not come back. Instead, a young man, not a soldier, whom Tabitha had often seen entering and leaving

Naaman's tent, unchallenged by the guards, came toward them. He was a pleasant, open-faced young man with startlingly blond hair and blue eyes. He seemed to be well known to the guards and with some authority, for as he approached they touched their foreheads in a gesture of respect. He spoke kindly to Tabitha and took her arm to lead her off, but again she clung tightly to Ulia. He spoke again, sharply this time, and to Ulia, but Ulia flung back her head in sudden defiance and enfolded Tabitha more closely in her tattered cloak.

The young man shrugged and nodded to the guard. Suddenly Tabitha found herself roughly torn from Ulia's clasp, her hands tied behind her, and a long leather thong fastened about her waist. Ulia's hands, too, were tied, and the leather thong fastened to her waist. So Tabitha understood that she was to march with the captives, but that she was not to be separated from Ulia. She turned gratefully to the young man, but he was looking curiously and with a slight smile into Ulia's snapping black eyes. Then he spoke commandingly to the guard, whose face suddenly turned defiant. He snapped his whip into the air with a mighty crack, but, as the young man spoke more sharply he sullenly folded it and tucked it into his leather belt. He shouted, and, one by one, the other guards, who had been busily tying up the rest of the captives, put away their whips with obvious reluctance. No whips today! Tabitha felt, rather than heard, the sigh that ran through the wretched group as the realization dawned upon them. But there was a great deal of shouting and prodding and wheeling of horses around them, and, since their pace was deliberate, no one stumbled or fell as they began their slow march down the plateau and on to the broad central street of the great city of Damascus.

Now that she was with Ulia, Tabitha had no more apprehensions about the future. She gazed in wonder at the lush gardens outside the town, and at the great bridge they crossed just before entering its walls. Crowds of people in colorful clothing lined the street. Up ahead she could hear their shouts and cheers as they greeted the victorious raiders, and the sound of trumpets as they neared the platform where the king himself awaited them. But she was unprepared for the sudden cascade of hatred and contempt that greeted the captives as they neared the crowds.There was hissing and spitting, rough shouts and derisive laughter. Once a clot of mud struck her shoulder and, frightened, she shrank closer to Ulia. But something had happened to Ulia. Whether it was the curious glance of the blond young man or the unwonted freedom from the dreaded whip, Tabitha could not guess. But in all that shuffling, cowering mob, only Ulia stood straight and tall and defiant. Her lips were moving. Suddenly Tabitha realized that she was singing, very softly at first, then, gaining courage, more and more loudly, until her neighbor heard and raised his head to join her. One by one, heads were lifted, shoulders raised, backs straightened; and the ancient song of the people of God began to swell above the tumult of the jeering crowd:

Hear, O kings; give ear, O princes;
to the LORD I will sing.
I will make melody to the LORD,
the God of Israel!

The jeers died in midair, and the shouts were hushed. Arms that were raised to fling dirt and debris suddenly dropped as if ashamed. Like a worm whose head can be distinguished from its tail only by the direction of its progress, the procession moved along with two seemingly triumphant heads. The guards, deprived of the punishing whips, soon stopped their wheeling playacting and rode quietly, if sullenly, beside their captives. Certainly there would be no attempts at escape, for this was one body, one cohesive group of worshipers whose God would not forsake them as they sang his praises in a strange land. And the people, from the smallest urchin to the king himself, watched and listened in amazement. They had seen many a captive people led in triumph through their streets, but never one that had itself so snatched victory out of degradation and defeat.

It did not last long. As soon as they had been herded into the small enclosure prepared for them and their bonds loosened, the bickering began: "Now it will go hard with us!" "Now they will really punish!" "What spirit possessed us to behave so defiantly?" "Now it will be the end!" "But our God must have heard, too, and he will be pleased!" "Better we should sing to him in Bethel or in Dan. Why could he not be pleased with us there?" "Who began this stupid chanting?" "What matters it who began? The spirit came on all of us, and I, for one, rejoice! It is a sign that the Lord God will not forsake us in our need." And Tabitha, who felt comforted and at home among all this bickering, laid her exhausted head in Ulia's lap and fell fast asleep.

She was awakened by a heavy hand on her shoulder. The guard again. Once more she clung to Ulia, but this time there seemed to be no question—they were to go together.

It was dusky evening; shouting and music still rang in the distance as the celebration continued. But the guard led them down narrow side streets and high-walled alleys and finally stopped before a narrow wooden door. They were admitted into a small court ablaze with cooking fires and astir with the going and coming of many men and women, all looking strangely alike in their short brown robes and leather belts. Tabitha guessed they were in the slaves' quarters of some great house. An old woman carrying a blazing torch led them into a small room. She slipped the burning torch into its socket on the wall, indicated the water for bathing and the clean clothing laid out on a bench, and left them.

Ulia sighed with pleasure as she slipped the rough homespun robe over her clean body and shook out her wet hair. Even Tabitha, who had never before been unduly concerned with the luxuries of cleanliness, felt refreshed. The robe she had been given was far too long, but Ulia showed her how to tuck it up around the leather belt so that she would not trip. Then they sat on the bench and waited for what was to come next.

The old woman returned and led them back into the court. She set Ulia to the task of shredding lentils into one of the great boiling pots, then took Tabitha by the arm to lead her away.

Tabitha shrank from her, but Ulia spoke, sharply for Ulia.

"Tabby, God has been good to us. We are safe here. But now you must go the way he has set for you, and you must not be afraid. He will be with you, and I think we will see each other often. Now go!"

There was too much to wonder at to be afraid. Through the arches of a colonnaded walk she glimpsed another court where masses of banked flowers sprang to life and color under the flaring torches set along the walls. In one corner a noisy little rivulet cascaded down a small pile of rocks among the flowers, passed under the tiniest bridge she had ever seen, and then simply disappeared among more rocks. How strange! And why a bridge where one could easily just step across? And how strange to build one's house *around* a stream instead of *beside* it, where the neighbors could share it's living refreshment!

But the old woman was hurrying her past the court down the arcaded walk to a heavily curtained doorway. She parted the curtains, thrust Tabitha through, and left her there, standing uncertain and alone.

It was a large apartment, shimmering in soft lamplight in shades of silken green and gold. The walls rustled slightly where drafts caught their woven hangings. Cushions were piled high on a bed in the corner, and the floor was soft and warm with animal skins. In the far corner the draperies were lifted, disclosing an adjoining room. The vibrating glow of live coals in a small brass container was reflected in the golden hair and blue garments of the woman seated near it. Beside her a young man was reading aloud from a manuscript. Tabitha recognized him. It was the young man who had ordered that she be allowed to remain with Ulia on the march into Damascus.

The woman turned as he stopped reading. It was obvious that they were mother and son, although her eyes held more of a misty grayness than his bright blue. But the golden hair, the slightly tilted nose, and the generous, smiling lips were all of the same piece.

"Come here, Tabitha!" The young man spoke in her own

tongue, although it sounded strangely different from his lips. As Tabitha approached, he went on: "My name is Melos. This is my mother, the lady Hiliah, the wife of Naaman, the captain of the king's armies, whom you have seen. She is to be your mistress; you will serve her and obey her, and in time, I know, you will come to love her, as we all do."

He spoke then to his mother, and Tabitha caught her name several times among the strange words.

Then the woman spoke. "Tabitha!" she said, and held out her hand. The smile was so gracious and the voice so warm that Tabitha felt no hesitation; she came close and knelt by her side; her mistress touched her black curls with a light caress, and Tabitha's heart was won. Henceforth she would be as eager to learn and as quick to serve as gratitude and affection could make her.

Her education began at once. Hiliah spoke to her in Syrian, and in a short while Tabitha realized that she was repeating the same phrase over and over. Hesitantly, Tabitha repeated the strange sounds. When she had conquered them perfectly, Hiliah raised her hand and pointed to the curtained doorway with an unmistakable gesture. And Tabitha went.

She did not see Uliah in the servants' court, but she found the old woman and repeated the unknown message. The shadow of a smile crossed the ancient face as she spoke to one of the women nearby. Soon Tabitha was presented with a small platter containing a dewy bunch of grapes, and again waved off. Once more she passed by the flowered court, but in the narrow arcade she met an unexpected problem. Striding ahead of her was the powerful, black-bearded figure of Naaman. She hesitated as she heard the welcoming voices greeting him beyond the curtain; then, not knowing what else to do, slipped in as unobtrusively as possible.

The soft fur at her feet betrayed her. As she stumbled and fell, she held the platter high to protect its burden, but as she and it clattered to the floor, the grapes flew with uncanny accuracy straight for Naaman's black-bearded cheek. With a savage roar he whirled, his sword already out of the scabbard, to face a foe that was mystifyingly not there. Melos ran forward and helped her to her feet, speaking to his father in a voice with a little laugh behind it. Naaman gave a great sigh, replaced his sword, and began to wipe the sticky remnants of the bruised and sodden grapes from his beard with the cloth Hiliah had given him, all the while regarding her with a dark frown above his sharp blue eyes.

Melos wasted no time. He handed her the platter, repeated the order his mother had given her, and pushed her out the door. Trembling, near to tears, Tabitha went again to the old lady in the servants' court. She looked at the child sharply, but supplied the grapes, and very carefully this time, Tabitha managed to deposit them safely upon the small table near Hiliah's chair.

Naaman seemed very tired. He had slumped into the chair Melos had vacated, and his son stood behind it. Hiliah knelt before him, loosening the bindings of his leather leggings. Melos spoke to her in his strange accent, and again with the little laugh behind the voice: "Tabitha, my father asks your pardon. He is accustomed to assault by spear and sword, but your attack by grape caught him completely unprepared. He wishes you well and hopes you will continue to serve the Lady Hiliah as best you can."

Tabitha forced her eyes upward to Naaman's face and saw, indeed, that there was a slight smile behind the beard, and the blue eyes twinkled a bit behind the fatigue. She had never before seen him without a helmet, and she was startled to see strange bands of gray in the black of his heavy hair. His forehead, too, was red and angry with painful looking sores, caused, she supposed, by the chafing of the helmet.

"Now," went on Melos, "you may take this mess"—and he handed her the stained and sticky cloth, inside which were wrapped the ruined grapes—"to old Zilchasta. She will show you what to do with it. Then come back. Outside the door you will find a small stool upon which you may sit until you are needed here."

Zilchasta frowned and shook her head. The remnants of the grapes were thrown into a basket near the outer door which, Tabitha learned later, contained other fragments of food provided for beggars. The cloth was thrown into a huge cauldron of boiling sudsy water at the other end of the court. The story of her mishap seemed to follow her through the court, and she was glad to escape the smiles and laughter and return to the little stool set outside the door of the lady Hiliah's apartments. She could hear voices from within—Melos', young, eager, laughing; Hiliah's, soft, gentle, warm, and loving; Naaman's, tired, infrequent, heavy with fatigue. She remembered his slumping figure, his gray-streaked hair and scabrous forehead. He seemed an altogether different person from the warrior who had caught her up onto his great horse and carried her off to this new life.

It was not a bad life. Tabitha's duties were light and her mistress undemanding. In time the terror and ache of her memories began to subside, and when Melos began to teach her to read and write, as well as to speak, the strange new language, she discovered an excitement in learning that might never have come her way in the poverty-stricken little village that had been her home in Samaria.

With Ulia it was different. She went about her duties obediently enough, but there was a pride in her straight back and a defiance in her smoldering eyes that set her vividly apart from the rest of those serving in Naaman's household. And sometimes when, in the evenings, Tabitha sat with the others around the dying fires in the servants' court listening to strange tales and ancient stories, Ulia would begin to sing. Her clear voice and vibrant rhythms were infectious, and soon those of the group who were Israelites joined in the ancient songs they had learned in their childhood. And sometimes, when the chants and melodies rose to near frenzied heights, Ulia would dance. As the lithe, graceful figure swayed and circled around the fires, the flickering light brought color to the dull brown robe, and Tabitha remembered. . . . The young people of the village were dancing around Ulia in the open square; their scarves and sashes flashed brilliant oranges, blues, and yellows as they wove dusty patterns in the sunlit air. Best of all, she was seated nearby in the shade of a fig tree, her mother on one side of her and her father on the other, and she felt happy and excited and never afraid. This memory did not fade as so many of her other memories had, and the empty ache within her was so great that she sometimes wished Ulia would not dance. Once, when she turned her head to hide the tears, she glimpsed Melos in the shadows, watching intently, a look on his face that puzzled and disturbed her. But then she saw Hiliah at his side and felt reassured. Ulia's dance *was* lovely to watch, though Melos and Hiliah could not possibly understand its meaning.

"Teach me your dance!" The young man caught Ulia's hand just as she was about to seat herself again beside Tabitha. He was an attractive young man, in spite of the shapeless brown slave robe he wore, and he came from a village not far from Tabitha's own, but a Canaanite village.

Laughing, breathing deeply from her exertions, Ulia shook her head. "I dance to the Lord," she said. "It is not for the heathen." She sank to the floor beside Tabitha.

"Heathen? What do you mean by 'heathen'? In my own land I worshiped Baal as devoutly as you your Lord God. I do not think of myself as a 'heathen.'" He half knelt beside them, balancing lightly on his toes. His name was Ephron, and Tabitha liked him.

"And whom do you worship here in Damascus?" asked Ulia.

"Rimmon, of course. Who else?"

"You see?" said Ulia. "You have no god, really. You change gods as easily as you change clothing. You are heathen!"

"But that is ridiculous!" Ephron seated himself more comfortably before them and picked up a straw from the dirt floor. "In Canaan Baal rules, and there I worship him. But in Damascus, Rimmon rules. How foolish it would be to depend on Baal in the land where Rimmon holds the power!"

"But our Lord God is different! He is *above* all other gods! He alone is God!" Ulia's conviction shone in her eyes and thrilled in her voice. "He does not rule in only one land. He created the world and holds power over the whole of it! He chose us to be his very own people because he loves us, and he rules wherever we are! He brought us out of slavery in Egypt. He opened up the Red Sea so we could cross over; he helped us while we wandered in the dreadful wilderness; and he brought us to the land he had promised us. There he made us a great people and nation, with powerful and glorious kings: David, Solomon. . . . " A shadow crossed her face, and she hesitated.

"And Ahab," Ephron finished for her, but he did not smile because of her pain, "who worshiped Baal!"

Ulia sighed. "Yes," she said simply.

"Ahab was wise," said Ephron, "and he acted wisely. Baal was the god of Canaan, long before your people invaded and conquered it. Baal did not lightly give up his power to your foreign Lord God, and Ahab prospered while he worshiped Baal. But now we hear that your present king . . . What is his name?"

"Jehoram," said Tabitha.

"Yes. Jehoram no longer worships Baal and has thrown down the sacred pillar of Baal that Ahab set up. And see what results. The Syrians, no longer bound by their treaty with Ahab, raid your country when they will, and Jehoram cannot stop them. And you are here in slavery, away from your home and your people. If your Lord God loves you, as you say, and is all powerful and rules wherever you are, why does he allow it? Why does he not save you?"

"He has a purpose," began Ulia, but Tabitha interrupted.

"Why does not Baal save *you*?"

Ephron shrugged easily. "Rimmon was stronger than Baal. So now I worship Rimmon. No," he went on, "that is where your belief in one all-powerful God breaks down completely. You have no explanation for evil when it comes your way."

"It is because of our sins," said Tabitha, who had learned the old lessons well.

Ephron turned to her with a half smile. "And what sins did you commit, little Tabitha? Did you murder someone? Did you steal some precious jewel from the temple of your God? What enormous wrong could you have done that your parents had to be murdered, your village burned, and you . . . "

"Enough!" cried Ulia sharply, for Tabitha had begun to cry. "You do not understand, and you will never understand!"

"No," said Ephron heatedly. "And you cannot explain it to me. You yourself do not understand your Lord God!"

"You are right," said Ulia slowly and more quietly. "I do not understand him or his ways. And yet I will trust him and worship him, and I will *not* teach you my dance. Come, Tabitha, let us go to bed." And as they turned toward the women's quarters, Tabitha caught sight of Melos' tall figure disappearing down the arcade, and knew that he had been listening as well as watching.

The next morning when she brought fresh water to her mistress, Melos was there and began to question her.

"Is it true, Tabitha, that you Israelites believe in only one God?"

"Oh, yes!" said Tabitha.

"That is a strange thing," said Melos. "And yet I have heard from someone, or perhaps read it, that there was once an Egyptian king who believed in only one god. Did your people not come from Egypt long ago?"

"Yes," said Tabitha. "We were slaves in Egypt, but the Lord God brought us out with a strong hand and a mighty arm, and brought us to our own land, where we lived until . . . "

Melos smiled. "You speak like a small poet, Tabitha!"

Tabitha nodded. "We have a song. My mother taught it to me. Ulia sings it sometimes, and I think you have heard her."

"Yes," said Melos hastily. "I have heard Ulia sing. But about this one only God. I suppose your people could have learned that from the Egyptians."

"Oh, no!" said Tabitha positively. "We have nothing to do with the gods of Egypt. Our Lord God told us himself that he was the one Lord."

"Your God spoke to you?" asked Melos incredulously.

"Yes, of course. On the fiery mountain. He said we were to

have no other gods but him, and we should love him with all our heart and soul and might."

"How very strange. Your God speaks to his people and asks them to love him? Our gods demand only fear and speak to us through priests whose oracles can be bought by the highest bidder. I must know more about your God."

"You should ask Ulia," said Tabitha eagerly. "She knows a great deal more than I, and she remembers the old songs."

"Ulia!" Melos sighed and rubbed his chin. "You know, Tabitha, Ulia is perhaps the loveliest slave ever captured and has probably the sharpest tongue. No, Tabitha, when I want to know about your God and your people, I will ask you. I am afraid of Ulia!" And the smile he gave her seemed somehow a little crooked.

"Does your Lord God still speak to his people?" he asked on another occasion. "Have you heard him?"

Tabitha shook her head. "He does not speak to us openly, as he once did on the fiery mountain. But we have prophets."

"Oh. Oh, yes! We have prophets, too, to whom our gods speak, if one can believe them. And the more money one pays the more pleasant the prophecies."

Tabitha shook her head again. "No, no!" she cried impatiently. "Our Lord God is not like that! He speaks to his prophets, and they tell us his will, and we do not pay them for it. Indeed, when Ahab ruled, hundreds of them had to hide in caves, and the great Elijah himself had to hide for years in the desert with nothing to eat but what the birds brought him. But he continued to speak God's will, and brought down fire from heaven to show the Lord God's power over Baal, and then brought rain after the great famine."

"I have heard Ulia tell the story. I might more likely believe it had she seen it herself."

"She was too young," said Tabitha. "But my father saw it. Our village is . . . was . . . " She drew a deep breath and went on, "It was not far from Mount Carmel, in the plain of Esdraelon. And when the people gathered on the mountain for the contest between Baal and our Lord God, my father went, too. He was just a boy, but he saw the fire from heaven."

"Now that is very strange. I thought Ulia's story of the fire from heaven had come from long ago, like the songs of Deborah and Jael that she likes to sing, and the stories of Moses and David. But your father actually saw it? Does this prophet still live? This Elijah?"

"No. Yes. That is . . . " Tabitha stopped in confusion.

"What do you mean, 'No, yes'?" Melos' sharp blue eyes held a laugh within them. "A man is either alive or he is dead. How can there be confusion on such a point?"

"He is alive," answered Tabitha slowly, "but not in Israel. Our Lord God took him up by a whirlwind into heaven, in a chariot and horses of fire."

Melos' laugh broke into her words. "So, after all, your superstitions are much the same as ours! Now Elijah is a god in his own right, I suppose, and demands your worship and obedience!"

"No, no, no!" Tabitha almost stamped her foot in her impatience. "You are trying not to understand! Elijah is with God and is no longer concerned about us. We have nothing more to do with him except to remember. But he cast his mantle upon Elisha, and his spirit came upon Elisha, and it is Elisha who is now the prophet of our Lord God. He has done great things and has even raised a child from the dead."

Melos raised his eyebrows. "There is one thing in which you Israelites excel beyond other people—your imagination! No man, not even a prophet of your Lord God, could raise . . . "

Naaman's sudden roar from the court outside sent Tabitha scurrying for the bowl of wilted flowers she had been sent to remove. As she dashed with them back to the servants quarters, Melos rose to greet his father.

Tabitha did not see—or even hear—much of Naaman in the daily course of her life. He was often gone for weeks at a time on military duties; but even when in Damascus, the king seemed in perpetual need of his services, so that if he was home at all, it was only late at night after Hiliah had dismissed her. Yet there was no mistaking the fact of his presence whenever he was there. He was never physically cruel or unkind to his servants, but his easily aroused anger and the roar of his voice—as often in laughter as in wrath—produced a tension that could be felt in even the farthest corners of his great house. Yet perhaps only she and old Zilchasta realized how completely his arrogance, his air of authority, and even his physical vitality drained away as soon as he entered the family apartments, and he became only a tired, aging, and sick old man. It was as though, before guests and servants, he must be always playacting a part that had once been natural to him, but became ever more difficult to maintain.

She was surprised whenever she saw him at how gray he had become, thinking always that she had not remembered how it had been the last time she had seen him. Yet the gray now seemed to be invading even the great black beard that had once frightened her so, and she wished it were not necessary for him so regularly to wear that chafing helmet.

Yet the realization of the nature of his illness did not dawn on her until the day he came in quietly from a three-months absence. Quietly. There was no more playacting. She had been fastening a jeweled comb into her mistress' hair, and she looked up in astonishment and shrank back in horror. She had seen a leper once, outside her native village, and the children had thrown stones at him and driven him away. Now here were the same snow-white hair and beard, the same scabrous sores on every exposed portion of his skin—his face and neck, his arms and hands, even his legs above the leather guards. But Lady Hiliah rose to greet him with nothing but compassion and concern for his welfare on her lovely face. Tabitha fled almost screaming into the arms of Ulia, who drew her aside to quiet her and learn the cause of her sudden terror.

"Ulia!" Her whisper was frantic. "He is a leper! Lord Naaman is a leper, and Lady Hiliah receives him and—and I have been in the same room with him—and—and—Ulia, what must I do?"

"Quiet, child, quiet!" soothed Ulia and held her close. "It is not as bad as you think."

Ephron came up, concerned. "Is she hurt? What is the trouble?"

"It is nothing." Ulia seemed almost embarrassed. "She will be all right. I must explain some things to her."

Zilchasta came up, a sardonic grin on her aged face. "You Israelites! I wondered how long it would be before the child realized. Send her back to her mistress at once!"

"In a moment." Ulia's black eyes snapped defiance, and Zilchasta withdrew.

"Tabitha," Ulia spoke quietly, but with great urgency. "Things are not the same here as in our own country. It is true that Naaman is a leper. I have known it for some time and should have warned you. But here there is not the same danger as we feel in Israel. I cannot explain it to you now, but you must trust me. You are in no danger from Lord Naaman or his illness. Here there is no sin or disgrace involved. Believe me, and go now and do your work. Later we will talk about it."

But Ulia had to use almost all her strength to disengage Tabitha's clutching arms, and it was only when the frowning Zilchasta once more bore down on them that she choked back her sobs and returned to her post. Hiliah was already calling for her, and as she was sent scurrying for warm water and ointments, for oil and wine and even for fresh flowers, the familiar motions of her duties eased the terror in her heart. And as she watched the tenderness and concern with which Hiliah and Melos attended Naaman, she felt within herself a compassion for this defeated old man who had once been so vital and powerful a warrior.

But the dread remained, and with it a growing bewilderment. How could a leper be so honored as to be commander of a king's armies, to live in so rich a house with his wife and son, and own slaves who, in her country, would have driven him out of their company with stones and sticks and curses?

"You Israelites are barbarians!" exclaimed Ephron that night around the dying fires. "Your Lord God orders you to treat a sick man so badly, and yet you claim he loves you? It is unbelievable!" And the Israelites among the slaves sat silent and ashamed, with no words to explain the unexplainable.

Yet Ulia spoke, slowly. "Our Lord God owes you no explanations, nor us. But for Tabitha's sake I will try to make you understand. Our Lord God created us to love him and to serve him, and it is only when we *do* so love him and serve him that we can be happy. For that is what we were created to do. But when we separate ourselves from him by our sin and disobedience, we can only be miserable and unhappy, for we have cut ourselves off from our source of love and happiness. But it is hard for us to remember that, because the temptation to sin is all around us, and seems so easy and pleasant. So our God has set for us a symbol—a sign to show how wretched and miserable we become when we cut ourselves off from him by our sin. That sign is leprosy. That is why any leper is cast out from among us because of his disease, just as we are cast out from our Lord God's presence when we sin. It is to show us our own misery that we make our lepers miserable."

"I understand fully." Ephron's voice was cold and hard. "Every time you drive a leper from your village streets you are saying within yourselves: 'So God drives me out from his presence because he loves me.' When your children throw sticks and stones, they are saying among themselves: 'We are showing our love to this poor, sick man, just as God shows his love to us by driving us away when we sin.' Is that the way it is?"

"No," said Ulia and bowed her head.

"Give me Baal or Rimmon every time! At least they do not pretend to love that which they so cruelly condemn." And he got up to walk away.

"But, Ulia," prodded Tabitha. "When our priests sacrifice, our sins are atoned for. Tell him!"

Ephron whirled. "And are your lepers cured when your sins are forgiven? Does your sacrifice atone for the symbol as well as for the fact? And when you sin again, does your cleansed leper return to his sores and his misery? Your God makes no sense!"

"No," said Ulia, humbly. "He makes no sense."

Tabitha was aghast. "But Ulia! There will come a prophet. Remember? Like Moses. He will explain all things."

"Will he also cure the lepers?" Ephron demanded hotly. "Show me one of your prophets who can heal a leper, and I will believe in a God who loves!"

That night Tabitha woke from her sleep and found she was sitting bolt upright on her mat. She was not sure whether she had actually screamed or done so only in her dream. But she was trembling violently, and a soft whimper escaped her as she bowed her head upon her knees. It had been a frightening dream, and she longed to wake Ulia for reassurance, but she did not. She lay down again, and every detail of the dream raced through her mind with terrifying clarity.

She was home, back in the little mud-brick house in the village in Samaria, and her mother and father, more vivid and real than her waking remembrance could picture them, were bending over her. They were crying, and gradually she realized that she was dead. She felt no fear, only a sadness that her parents were mourning and unhappy. Then she felt another presence in the room, and she turned her dead eyes toward him. He was old and bald, with a great flowing white beard and a glow about him that suggested more than merely human powers. He touched her hand, and she felt a rush of life and joy through all her body, and she rose and danced out into the sunshine. The children were there and all the young people dancing around Ulia in the square. But when she tried to join them, they shrank away from her, all except Ulia. Ulia held in her hand a heavy stick and, waving it threateningly before her, began to drive Tabitha out of the square. The children, too, began to taunt her and to pick up stones to throw at her as she turned to run. She could feel the skin of her face and arms drying up and becoming sore and encrusted, and knew that her black curls were turning white. As she stumbled through the dusty streets and away from the village, the thought came to her: "He raised me from the dead; could he not have cured me of this leprosy?"

For a long time she lay there trembling, and more than once she ran her fingers over her forehead and down her arms to feel the smooth, firm, healthy skin beneath her hand. She wondered why she did not tell Ulia of her dream, even when they rose in the morning. But there was forming in her a resolve, and she knew that Ulia would not approve. Ulia would not be convinced. But as the morning wore on, Tabitha became more and more certain of her way. Else why had God sent her such a dream?

Her heart was beating violently, but she tried to make her voice casual as she fastened her mistress' sandals: "I wish my Lord Naaman could go to the prophet who lives in Samaria; he could cure him of his leprosy."

Hiliah did not move, and after a long moment Tabitha dared to look up. Her mistress sat rigid, scarcely breathing, her face drained of all color, old and unlovely. Then the color came back; she leaned forward and took Tabitha's chin in her hand as her gray eyes bored into the child's.

Her voice was no more than a whisper: "How can you say something so—so ridiculous, so impossible?"

Tabitha did not shrink before her gaze. Her voice trembled, but she said stubbornly: "He raised a child from the dead; why should he not cure leprosy?"

Tabitha had never seen her mistress move so quickly. She almost threw Tabitha's face from her grasp, rose to her feet, and flew to the parting in the draperies that led to the inner chambers. Almost immediately Melos came in, his face concerned, his blue eyes sharp and unbelieving.

"What are you saying, Tabitha? Is this another of your legends? Do you know what you are talking about? Has your prophet really cured leprosy?"

"I do not know." Tabitha's courage was beginning to fail. "I only know he raised a child from the dead. Why should he not cure leprosy?"

"And if he can, will he?" Hiliah, hands clasped tightly before her and her face an agony, came to stand beside her son as his probing, insistent voice went on.

"Why should he heal a Syrian when there must be dozens of Israelite lepers on whom he could work his magic? Why should he even receive a man of our city who worships another god? What makes you think . . . "

"Leave her alone!" Naaman's deep, tired voice spoke from the parted curtain. In spite of herself, Tabitha drew back at the sight of his disfigured body. "She is only a child, with a child's imagination. You are only disturbing yourselves with the impossible. Send her off to her work and forget her wild imaginings!"

"But my lord, if there is a possibility?" Hiliah's gentle voice trailed off into nothingness.

There was a trace of harshness under Naaman's weariness. "Have I not had the king's own doctors, the best in Syria, at my service? Have not the priests of Rimmon interceded for me at the king's own command? Yet here I stand, consumed by this loathsome thing. And you grow excited over the wild fancies of a child slave. It is ridiculous! Speak no more of it!"

They stood silent, tense, even Naaman reluctant, in spite of his words, to quench the sudden, faint hope. Then Melos spoke sharply:

"Tabitha, fetch Ulia!"

Bewildered, half frightened, yet with head high and eyes defiant, Ulia stood before them, while Tabitha shrank as far as she dared against the curtained walls. Melos tried to soften the sharpness of his questioning.

"Don't be frightened, Ulia. We only wish you to tell us more about your prophet."

"Prophet, my lord? We have many prophets."

"Yes, of course. Tell us of the one who cures leprosy."

"I have not heard that any of our prophets have cured leprosy, my lord."

"But there is one who raised a child from the dead?"

"Yes, my lord. His name is Elisha. He has done great wonders among our people."

"Whose child did he heal?" interrupted Hiliah. "Some king's

son? A great lord or a wealthy man who could pay him well? We have gold and silver. . . . "

Ulia shook her head. "A woman of Shunem who had been kind to him. She was wealthy, but she did not pay to have her son restored. It is the Spirit of our Lord God who works through Elisha, and he does not require payment. His gifts are free."

"Can he heal leprosy?" Melos' probing voice began again.

"I do not know."

"Tabitha seems to think that he can. Has he ever tried?"

"I do not know."

"You are sure he has never done so?"

Ulia shook her head. "Such stories travel quickly among the people, my lord. I would have heard of it if it had been so."

"Even here in Damascus?"

"I often go marketing for Zilchasta, and there are tradesmen from our country. They tell us many things, but never that the prophet Elisha has healed a leper."

"Very well, Ulia. You may go." But when Tabitha began to follow, he called her back. His voice was angry.

"Tell me, Tabitha, why you seem to know so much more about your prophet than Ulia does? What makes you say that he can heal leprosy?"

"Let her be! The child wishes me well, and I am grateful. Now let us forget this fantasy, this wishful thinking!"

"But," faltered Tabitha, "my dream was so real."

"Dream?" Hiliah only half whispered it, but the two men tautened like bowstrings.

Melos sank slowly into Hiliah's chair. His effort at self control was almost visible, as if he found himself unexpectedly handling something as fragile as a soap bubble.

"Tabitha, tell us about your dream."

Relieved at the returned gentleness in his voice, Tabitha drew a deep breath. "I was dead, and the prophet brought me back to life. But I was a leper, and the people drove me out. I thought: 'He raised me from the dead; could he not have cured me of this leprosy?' And when I woke, I thought: Perhaps God has sent me this dream so that I could tell you. And—and then my Lord Naaman could go to Elisha and be healed."

"How do you know it was Elisha? Have you ever seen him?"

Tabitha shook her head. "No. But in my dream I knew it to be Elisha."

"Thank you, Tabitha. You may go now."

Slumped in the chair, legs outspread, he watched her go from under thoughtful brows. A few feet away, the gracious lady and the diseased man looked to their son as if for direction.

"Dreams are from the gods," murmured Hiliah tentatively.

"Dreams are dreams!" said Naaman harshly. "It means only that the child thinks leprosy and death are one and the same thing, and she is not far wrong." But he did not turn to leave them.

"Father," said Melos at last, rising to his feet. "Go to the king. He will surely give you a letter to the king of Israel and help you find Elisha. We will present ourselves to him, and we will bring gifts. I will go to the money changers, and, mother . . . "

"I will go to the bazaars," breathed Hiliah. "I will buy festal garments, the finest of our Damascene silks."

"No!" said Naaman.

Stunned, they stared at him.

"My lord," protested Hiliah. "You have nothing to lose."

"There is very little in this life that I still care about winning or losing," said Naaman. "But one thing I still possess—my self respect. What a fool I should look to go begging to a prophet of a strange God in a strange land—all at the word of a child slave—and come back as I went, unhealed! I will not risk such humiliation!"

"What you call self respect,"—there was ringing steel in Hiliah's usually soft voice—"is pride. Pride in your health and vigor, which is gone. Pride in your reputation as a warrior and hero, which will soon be forgotten. Pride in your position as commander of the king's army, which you cannot maintain for very much longer. Pride in your wealth and your family, which will mean less and less to you as you sink into the final miseries of your disease. If you do not care to be a fool in very truth, go to Israel!"

Each phrase snapped like a lash, and Melos felt almost surprised that his father did not physically wince at the blows. Instead, there seemed to be the ghost of a smile forming within the whitened beard, and Naaman laughed. It was only the echo of his former joyous shout, but, nevertheless, it was a laugh.

"Hiliah," he said, "I have never yet found the courage to oppose you when when you are angry. And what you say is true. I go to the king."

Two days later, in the predawn light of flaring torches, the procession started on its way. It was an impressive sight. A closed chariot for Naaman, wherein he might find what rest he could; an open chariot for Melos and the king's courier; pack camels carrying the gold and silver and silks that were to buy the foreign God's favor; soldiers on restless horses to guard the small caravan—and even Ephron. Late the night before, Hiliah had summoned him, ordered for him more appropriate clothing and a horse, and given him a special commission: "When it is known, one way or the other, do not wait for whatever ceremonies must conclude the matter. Come back at once and bring us the news, whether good or bad. I must be prepared, and the household."

To Ulia it was incredible. "Ephron, you will be going home!" She looked carefully about for anyone that might overhear. There was none but Tabitha, her little shadow. "You can escape. No one will follow you. You can be free again. You will be a fool if ever you come back here!"

Ephron's teasing grin lit up his face. "The Lady Hiliah is very observant," he said. "She knows that I will be back!" He laughed, and Tabitha wondered at the sudden color that flooded Ulia's face. "Besides," he went on more soberly, "I have made a promise concerning prophets who can heal lepers. I hope you will help me to keep it, if it needs to be kept."

Tabitha shrieked out farewells as the procession got under way, but Ulia was more apprehensive. "It is not the way to approach our Lord God, with gold and silks. But what could I do?

Tabitha!" She turned to her small niece, and the uneasiness in her eyes and voice bordered on anger. "Do you realize what you have done? There will be no fury like the fury of Naaman should he return unhealed and tricked!"

The days were long and empty. Half a dozen times Hiliah called for one or the other of her servants to accompany her to the temple of Rimmon for sacrifices and prayers, but halfway there she changed her mind and returned home. She questioned Tabitha endlessly about the Lord God of her country, and Ulia too. They told her what they could, but the reassurances she demanded of them they could not give. It was hard for her to accept the fact that neither coercion nor bribery, neither gifts nor merit, could move the Lord God of Israel to act favorably on any human request. Only love—and who could know whom the Lord God would choose to love? And how would the proud Naaman receive such a gift of love for which he could not pay? For which he could not even claim a certain merit, having been one of those who had pitilessly and frequently raided the country of the Lord God and killed and enslaved his chosen people?

"Would it move your Lord God to compassion," she asked, "if I were to set free all those in my household who are of his people?"

A sudden longing for the olive groves and barley fields of her country almost conquered Ulia. They could be gone and far away in their own hills and villages before Naaman could return, if she so insisted. But she shook her head.

"We do not bargain with our Lord God," she said. "We only submit ourselves to his will."

"Submit!" Hiliah was at last moved to anger. "Who are you to speak of submission? Have I not seen, day after day and month after month, the defiance in your eyes and the pride in the tilt of your head as you go about your duties? There is no submission or humility in you, and you are well aware of it. Do you have any realization of the treatment you might have received in any household but mine? That would have taught you real humility and submission."

Ulia bowed her head and closed her eyes, which she knew even now to be flashing with rebellion.

"I know, my lady. And do not think I am not grateful. But I beg you to remember I was born free, and it is not easy . . . " Her voice failed for a moment. Then her head lifted in the familiar proud tilt, and she did not check it. "Nevertheless, my lady, you must acknowledge, in all fairness, that however much I may rebel within myself, I *do* perform my duties, and I perform them well!"

"Because you fear the whip!"

"Because I fear my Lord God! And—yes—the whip too. But you, my lady, also fear to use the whip!"

Hiliah sank down into her chair and sighed deeply. "I need my men about me to help me laugh!" she mourned.

"Yes, my lady," said Ulia, and the half-smiles they exchanged were rueful acknowledgment of their own inadequate independencies.

Ephron arrived early one evening just as the cooking fires were dying down after the evening meal. He entered rather quietly and walked across the court. It was not until he was sure every eye was intent upon him that he finally spoke. He flung up both arms in a wild, exultant gesture and cried: "All praise and highest honor to the Lord, the God of Israel!" He flashed Ulia a jubilant grin and disappeared down the arcade toward Lady Hiliah's apartments.

Tabitha snatched up a small brass vase, plucked a few hurried blooms from the flowering inner court, stuffed them awkwardly into the vase, and followed Ephron through the curtained doorway.

Hiliah was sitting in her chair, pale and exhausted, eyes closed, as if in overwhelming relief. Tears slid down her cheeks as she bowed her head and murmured: "He is a great God, the Lord God of Israel!" Then she roused herself and dashed away the tears.

"Now you must tell me everything, from the very beginning. But you must be tired. Tabitha, bring up that stool for Ephron, and then you may go. No, no, of course you may stay.

Come here beside me, and we will listen together to what your Lord God has done. Now, Ephron, from the very beginning. What happened after the king sent for the prophet?"

Ephron hesitated a moment. "The king did not send for the prophet, my lady. In fact, he seemed very suspicious of us at first. There was talk—I was with the servants, as you know, my lady, and servants talk a great deal—there was talk that the king of Israel feared that King Benhadad had sent us with our request in order to stir up trouble, to start a quarrel that would give Syria an occasion for war against Israel. It frightened me greatly. The king of Israel has some mighty men of war at his court. But I do not know whether my lord Naaman was aware of the talk, though he chafed at the delay. Finally, a messenger arrived—a servant of the prophet, apparently—and we followed him to the prophet's dwelling. It was a small house, as simple as those surrounding it, and our company crowded the narrow street. People from all over the town, it seemed, were coming to stare at us and wonder. But the prophet's servant went directly into the house and came back almost immediately. The servant told me—I happened to be nearest—'Tell him, "Go and wash in the Jordan seven times, and your flesh shall be restored, and you shall be clean."' Then he returned to the house and closed the door.

"I was almost as angry over this discourtesy as I knew my Lord Naaman would be; yet I had to tell him. And, indeed, he was furious, as my lady can well imagine."

"I can, indeed!" Hiliah smiled faintly. "And yet—well?"

Ephron shook his head. "No, my lady. He gave orders that we turn back at once, shouting that the waters of Abana and Pharpar in his own country were a good deal cleaner and clearer than any of the filthy waters of Israel, including the Jordan, and he might rather wash in them and be clean.

"But we did, of course, have to cross the Jordan. At Dothan he gave orders that we take the northern route past Chinnereth, rather than crossing at Beth-shean, as we had come. But it was late, so we made camp on the plain at Dothan. And as we worked, it came to me that perhaps he was delaying the crossing in order that he might yet change his mind and do as the prophet had said. And since I—I have been very eager myself to believe on the Lord God of the Israelites, if he could show strength beyond that of Baal or Rimmon—I gathered up what courage I could and asked admittance to his tent. He was very weary and seemed asleep, but young Lord Melos received me.

" 'What are we to do?' he asked softly. 'He pouts like a small child. Of course, he expected something spectacular, like the fire from heaven, or at least that the prophet should come to him and openly call on the name of the Lord his God and wave his hands about to heal him. But simply to wash in the Jordan, like a peasant!' "

"Yes," said Hiliah. "It would be too humiliating. I hope that foolish pride of his will not some day utterly destroy him! Go on!"

"My Lord Naaman had stirred and opened his eyes while Melos was talking.

" 'So, Ephron,' he said. 'Is that what you will report to the Lady Hiliah, that I lie here and sulk like a spoiled child?'

"His voice was so weak that I made bold to approach his bed. 'My lord,' I said, 'if the prophet had given you some hard thing to do, such as . . . ' I could think of nothing, but Melos broke in.

" 'Yes, Father,' he said, 'suppose the prophet had told you to climb Mount Hermon and wash in its snows. Would you not have done so, weak as you are? And rejoiced in the challenge to cure yourself by your own exhausting effort? How much rather, then, when he says to you, "Wash and be clean"?'

"Naaman shook his head. 'I cannot believe it!' he said. 'How can any god's blessings come so easily? No sacrifice, no offering, no effort. As if all one needed to do was to accept them?'

" 'My lord,' I said. 'I have heard much from Ulia concerning the God of the Israelites. Might he not know that for you to do an easy thing and to trust him would be harder than to climb to the snows of Hermon?'

"He lay quietly for a few moments, while Melos and I scarcely dared to breathe. Then he sat up.

" 'How far are we from the Jordan?' he asked, and his voice was already stronger.

" 'About an hour's ride, my lord,' I said.

" 'The sun will not set before then,' he said. 'We will go!'

"I wanted to give a great shout, but did not dare. I turned to Melos, but he was already outside, giving orders to break camp. Nevertheless, Lord Naaman was too impatient even to wait until the carriages were set up, and we three started for the Jordan on horseback, giving the others orders to follow as soon as possible.

"I think my Lord Naaman must have suffered greatly during that hour's ride, for we rode furiously. So it was probably less than an hour when we reached the river. My Lord Naaman drove his horse directly up to its brink and virtually threw himself off it and straight into the water. Melos plunged in immediately after, for there was no ford here and the water was swift. Melos found a handhold on a clump of willows that grew on the bank and extended over the water. With the other hand he clung to his father and was almost submerged every time Naaman plunged into the depths. Lord Naaman allowed himself scarcely more than a breath each time he surfaced—that and a count of the number in a voice that grew ever stronger until at the seventh dip he was shouting in the old roar we had not heard for so long.

"In spite of the discomfort and strain, Melos was laughing like a child at a celebration; and when at last Naaman strode ashore we could both see the wonder. His skin was as smooth as a child's and his hair and beard had darkened almost to what it had been before. I say 'almost,' my lady, because, though the disease was gone, the suffering and despair of these past years had aged him somewhat. But the old vigor and excitement radiated from him as he began to strip off his wet clothes. Since I was the only one with any dry clothing among us, I gave him my cloak. He wrapped himself in it, and a great and pleasant weariness seemed to overtake him. I suppose, too, he has not slept well in years. He lay down on the soft meadow grass, but before he slept he said to me: 'Go and tell Lady Hiliah that there is no God in all the earth but in Israel.' So I left them there, my Lord Naaman asleep, and Melos watching over him."

Hiliah gave a great sigh. "'There is no God in all the earth but in Israel.' I will remember that all my life."

"I too, my lady," said Ephron.

"He will have gone back to the prophet today," she said thoughtfully, "to thank him and to offer his gifts, and will not begin the journey home till tomorrow. A two-day journey; then we will thank the God of Israel with a celebration such as this house has never known before! But you, faithful Ephron, you have not slept?"

"I rode through the night, my lady, stopping only for food and drink, and to change horses, as you instructed, at Aphek and Geshur."

"You shall be rewarded. You and Tabitha. I do not know what Lord Naaman will offer, but, at the least, I think you will be given your freedom, with enough funds for whatever you will need to establish yourselves again in your own country. Would that please you, my dear little Tabitha?"

Bewildered, Tabitha stared at her mistress and then turned helplessly to Ephron. His pleasant face turned suddenly cold and hard.

"May I remind the Lady Hiliah that Tabitha's parents are dead, her village burned, her people scattered or murdered, and that she has no one to care for her in her own country."

Hiliah bowed her head and covered her eyes with her hands. It was with almost a shudder that she murmured: "May the God of Israel forgive us for what we have done to his people!" Then she stood up decisively. "I shall insist that all in our household who worship Israel's God shall be set free, and Lord Naaman will agree. Surely, there will be some among them who will care for you, Tabitha."

"Ulia, I will go with Ulia," faltered Tabitha.

Hiliah smiled. "Oh, yes. Ulia. She has never been less than free, though she does not know it. Now go, Ephron. Get food and rest. You have done me a great service, and I shall not forget it."

Ephron hesitated, seemed about to speak, thought better of it, and left them.

"Dear little Tabitha," murmured Hiliah, dropping back into her chair. "I shall miss you. And I think you will miss me a little, too. Is that why you look so troubled? Perhaps I could even persuade you to stay. But you will be a woman soon, and it will be better for you in your own land and among your own people."

"Yes, my lady." But Tabitha's face did not clear, and to cover her own emotion, Hiliah spoke a little sharply.

"Child, what are you doing with that wretched little bunch of wilted flowers? Go immediately and fetch some fresh ones. And this time," there was laughter in her voice, "there is no great hurry. Take a little time to give them some water!"

By the time Tabitha had gathered and arranged the flowers, she knew what she must say: "My lady, do you know that Ephron is not an Israelite? He worships Baal and Rimmon. If he does not go, neither will Ulia. And I must stay with Ulia; I have no one else."

But Hiliah was lying exhausted on her bed when Tabitha returned, apparently sound asleep. She set the flowers quietly on the little table and went out.

She started back toward the servants' court, where the evening singing was beginning. Ephron must have finished his somewhat shortened account and there would be great rejoicing. He probably would have said nothing about the Israelites being freed. That would have to wait till Naaman himself came to confirm it. He was not the kind to arouse false hopes—particularly when his own position was so unclear. Nevertheless, there would be rejoicing, and Ulia would dance to the Lord her God, the God of Israel, who had worked so wondrous a miracle. As she passed from the arcade into the court, Tabitha stopped suddenly and her face cleared.

The dancing had indeed begun. Amid the glowing lights and shadows of the dying fires were not one, but two swaying figures. Ulia was teaching Ephron her dance, and all would be well. (This story is based on the Biblical account given in 2 Kings 5:1-14.)

Pearls for a King

Not within the memory of living man had the little village of Bethlehem sheltered so many guests. The chill wind that swept in fitful gusts down the narrow lanes and alleys carried on its breath the talk and laughter of strange men. David's children had come to David's town to be numbered and taxed by the usurper of David's throne. Every chamber in the village held its tiny lamp glowing in some traveler's honor.

Below the caverned cliffs that marked the eastern end of the village, the courtyard of the little khan was alive with unusual activity. Its drab stone walls echoed to the clatter of burros' hooves, the cry of the muleteers, the chatter of serving maids, and the talk and laughter of brightly robed guests.

From the curtained doorway on the second floor that marked the entrance to the guest rooms emerged a little serving girl, clad in a faded brown robe. A moment she paused on the landing, then carefully picked up a small stone water jar, swung it to her shoulder, and descended the open stairs to the courtyard. Directly behind the stairs and beneath the guest rooms was a large natural cavern opening into the cliff. Here, on a raised platform, were the clay ovens, caldrons, basins, and bowls used in the preparation of food for the guests. Here, too, were the large pots in which was stored sufficient water for the day's use. With a small gourd the girl began to dip water from a pot into her jar. To the left and behind her the cave stretched far under the cliff, providing ample room for the innkeeper's cattle and the pack animals of the guests.

In a sheltered corner of the courtyard two shepherds, leaning on their long crooks, watched the scene with interest. The younger caressed between his fingers the two coins they had received in payment for the crippled lamb they had brought, and which was even now being slaughtered for supper underneath the steps.

"It would have brought us five times this amount if we had waited for the Temple commissioner," he complained.

The older man shook his head. "It would never have passed inspection. You know that, Eliud."

"They are all against us," said Eliud bitterly. "The emperor lays on us a new tax, and the priests at Jerusalem insist on perfection in the lambs for sacrifice. Who can insure perfection at every birth? And who concerns himself with the poor shepherd? He pays more and receives less, and God only knows how we shall live!"

"He has always provided us with our needs."

"Yours, Jacob. Not mine!"

"Forgive me, Eliud!" Jacob laid a gnarled hand on the younger man's arm. "You do, indeed, have greater needs than mine. Your Rachel—she is no better?"

Eliud shrugged. "In body well enough. But her spirit—no, there is no spirit left in her!"

"How long is it since the death of the child?"

"Two years. Two years since I have heard her laugh or seen her smile—she who was once so full of laughter and joy, till I took the dead child from her arms. Now she wanders silently from place to place in our small home, often bringing out and folding and refolding the clothes in which our newborn son would have been swaddled had he lived. Once I tried to take them from her. I will not do it again!"

"She mourns beyond understanding! But it is your sorrow, too!"

Eliud sighed. "Yes. There is no joy in my homecoming. She speaks but a word now and then when I question her directly. Otherwise there is a circle of silence around the two of us, beyond which the chatter of her mother's sister Hadassah seems to swirl like dead autumn leaves. Sometimes I feel we would do better without the old woman, and yet I dare not leave Rachel alone. She clings to me when I leave. Yet a man must earn bread for his family—and for the Emperor's tax!" This last was spoken with such bitter venom that Jacob cast a frightened glance about them.

"Quiet, man! We are not out in the fields with only the silly sheep to hear!"

"Don't worry! Those Romans are too busy with their wineskins to concern themselves about two lowly Judean shepherds! But you too are a son of David. Do you not feel bitterness that these usurpers of David's throne take the last shekel from David's people so that the Emperor in Rome may build a new palace or present his latest harlot with expensive jewels? Where is God with his promises that David's house should rule forever? Why do we suffer this shame, and where is our deliverer?"

"Sometimes I feel he may be closer than we know." The old shepherd's faded eyes wandered past the terraced olive groves on the darkening hills to the first faintly twinkling star above. "Our father Jacob said the scepter should not depart from our people until the Christ comes. And the scepter is long gone. What further proof do we need that the time is near?"

"Near? Perhaps in the thousand years that are as a day in the sight of the Lord! Meanwhile we suffer! Do you know, Jacob, that in the last year I have laid aside, by frugal living, some few paltry shekels in the wretched hope that some day I should be able to save enough to take Rachel to Alexandria. There is a physician there, Eleazer the priest tells me, by name of Philip, who has had some success in healing sicknesses of the mind. But now almost half of what I have must go for this new tax! How old will Rachel be before we reach Alexandria? And how far will her mind have slipped away through all those years of loneliness and sorrow? Could even Philip of Alexandria bring her back after so long a time? Provided, of course, that Philip of Alexandria will treat a poor shepherd's wife for the price of a crippled lamb!" He clacked the two pieces of coin together in his palm and then thrust them into his pouch.

"Cast your care upon the Lord," said Jacob softly, "for he cares for you!"

"Ah, yes, the Lord! At your age, Jacob, you should surely have learned that the Lord has no love for the poor. It is the rich and the usurer that he favors, and—oh, yes—the innkeeper!"

Eliud's sullen eyes rested on the paunchy figure of the innkeeper who appeared at that moment on the landing above, trying to shield the futile glow of his lamp from the wind. On his face was a look of benign satisfaction. His rooms were full; the little leathern bag under the cushion in his chamber was heavy with copper and even some silver. A few more such days and he could purchase that vineyard of Isaac ben Zadok that he had coveted so long.

At the bottom step the innkeeper paused in sudden astonishment. The watching shepherds turned to follow his gaze. Four Ethiopian slaves, bearing on their stalwart shoulders a large, heavily curtained litter, entered the gate. Their short tunics fluttered in the wind, and the broad bands of gold on their arms contrasted vividly with the ebony of their skin. Behind them trailed four or five heavily laden burros and a muleteer.

The innkeeper rushed forward. Ben Zadok's vineyard? Surely, that and a new winepress, too! The lamp in his hand came near to being shattered in his excitement. Every eye in the courtyard was fixed on this imposing sight, and every tongue was hushed.

Expertly the slaves lowered the litter and gently set it down. The heavy curtains parted.

"Peace to you!" The resonant voice reached even the two shepherds in the far corner.

"And p-prosperity to you!" stuttered the trembling innkeeper.

"Have you rooms for myself and for my daughter? We have come from far, and my daughter is weary."

"Indeed, sir!" The innkeeper made no attempt to conceal his eagerness. "For you and your daughter we will make room! Leah!" he called sharply to the little serving girl. "Hurry and tell your mistress to prepare the south rooms for our guests." In a hurried undertone he added: "Those who have hired them are gone into the village. Remove their things. Put them into the storeroom. I will arrange with them later. Hurry!"

Like a swallow Leah skimmed up the narrow stairs and vanished.

Meanwhile a man, the like of whom the shepherds had never seen before, stepped out of the litter. His tall, lithe figure seemed young, yet above his soft brown beard his large eyes held the wisdom and compassion of maturer years. His cloak was of heavy, richly embroidered wool, and as he straightened himself, the rays of the innkeeper's lamp caught the gleam of a jewel in his turban.

"Had I that man's money!" muttered Eliud under his breath.

"Elam! Dan!" shouted the innkeeper back into the cavern. "You dull-witted fools! Unload these animals, and bring the master's things to the south rooms. Hurry now!"

The two boys, fingers nimble in the hope of reward, began to help the muleteer unload the various bags and baskets tied to the burros, as the innkeeper turned again to the stranger.

"It will be only a few moments, sir, until the rooms are ready. They are humble, but warm, and you will be comfortable. Will you enter?"

The stranger turned to the litter and lifted the curtain.

"Come, Naomi," he said gently. "Here we will rest. Wrap your cloak closely about you, child, for it is cold."

Deliberately, with the conscious grace of one early trained in social behavior, a young girl stepped down from the litter. Her slender body was muffled in a cloak of heavy, bright blue wool, richly lined and trimmed with silk. As she took her father's arm and followed the beaming innkeeper, she turned her head neither to the right nor to the left, as became a modest maiden; but her eyes, frankly young and curious, wandered where they would. With difficulty she smothered a most undignified giggle as she spied the two shepherds gazing at her in openmouthed astonishment. A sudden gust of wind whipped up the corner of her headdress, revealing a necklace of dull gold and pearls, the rich gleam of which made Eliud catch his breath. She fingered it lovingly; it was a birthday gift from her father, and she could hardly be persuaded to lay it aside, even at night.

As the little group disappeared into the upper rooms, Jacob became suddenly aware of the gathering darkness. The Ethiopians had carried the litter into the far corner of the courtyard, and, arrogant in their strange splendor, had gathered around the fires in the cavern entrance, grateful for their warmth against the oncoming night.

"We must go," began Jacob, but cut his sentence short as his attention was attracted by another couple entering the courtyard gates. These were humble people, their simple clothing stained with the dust of many days' travel. The man led a small burro upon which the woman was riding into the center of the court. He looked about him uncertainly.

"Help me down, Joseph," said the woman softly.

"Of course." Her husband turned to help her. "Are you tired, Mary? Surely, they will let us stay here. It is almost night."

Mary slid awkwardly from her seat and stood unsteadily, half leaning against the animal at her side.

Joseph was about to approach the servants gathered about the fires in the cavern when he spied little Leah coming down the steps.

"Child, is your master here—the innkeeper? I must speak with him."

"He is coming directly. But I think he will have no room for you." She eyed Mary curiously, then ran off to join the servants.

For long minutes they waited, silent, almost motionless. The gay chatter about the fires continued unconcernedly. In all that busy court none, except perhaps old Jacob, paid any heed to this insignificant couple.

At length the innkeeper, still smiling to himself, descended the stairs.

"Have you a room, innkeeper, where my wife may rest?" inquired Joseph, advancing a few steps. "We have come from far, and she is in great need."

"No," said the innkeeper, scarcely glancing at Joseph. "Our rooms are already crowded. Even the courtyard is filled—as you can see for yourself. There is no room."

"But sir," protested Joseph, "My wife needs shelter, a bed."

The innkeeper glanced a second time at the strained face and weary figure of the woman standing beside the burro. But again he shook his head.

"I am sorry. But it is impossible. Perhaps you can find shelter with one of the townspeople."

"No, Joseph!" interrupted Mary faintly, but intensely. "I cannot go farther. We must stay here."

"But woman," the innkeeper frowned, "there is no place, I tell you! Can I cast out one of my paying guests for you? It cannot be, I say!"

Silently they stood there, Mary with drawn face and closed eyes, Joseph looking helplessly from her to the adamant innkeeper. In his corner old Jacob glanced sidewise at Eliud, half expecting another tirade against the rich. But Eliud was seeing nothing. His gaze was still fastened on the arch in the upper story through which the rich man and his daughter had gone.

A tug at her robe aroused Mary. The child Leah stood at her side. With her she had brought one of the maid servants, capable and strong, who now gently took Mary's arm.

"Come with me," she said. "The stable is warm and dry, and the straw is clean. I will help you!"

"Yes, Sarah!" The innkeeper was manifestly relieved over this solution to the problem. "Take care of her. For a while we can manage without you. Go!"

As the trio, followed by the plodding burro, disappeared behind the fires into the recesses of the cavern, Jacob roused himself.

"Come, Eliud!" He spoke a bit irritably. "Stop your dreaming and let us go. It is almost night, and the others will be waiting for us."

Eliud turned slowly and looked at Jacob with unseeing eyes.

"Asa, my nephew, will watch in my place," he said unsteadily. "He is young, but faithful. I will send him to you. I am afraid for Rachel and will stay with her tonight."

Through the frosty silence of midnight Eliud cautiously made his way down the steeply terraced slopes of the easternmost hills of Bethlehem. The wind had dropped, and the stars shone in unnumbered brilliance in the moonless heaven. The path he was pursuing would, he knew, take him to a cleft in the rock where, with a little careful climbing, he could enter unnoticed the cavern behind the inn.

It was not till he had safely entered the stable that he noticed a light, faintly illuminating a far corner of the cavern. It startled him, and he was half minded to turn back when, over the hushed munching and breathing of the oxen, he heard the vibrant cry of a baby, echoing strangely against the rocky walls. Then he remembered the couple that had come to the inn that evening. They had asked for a room, he recalled, and had been sent to the stable. He had forgotten them.

But there was no need for them to interfere with his plans. A score of men could hide here in this enormous cavern and know nothing of each other's presence. Still, it would be safer to know whether the couple were alone with their newborn child or the serving maid was still with them. Furtively he crept toward the light, cautious that his shadow should not emerge from the darkened walls and betray him.

A few yards from the feeble light he found a jagged niche in the rock from which he could safely observe the little group. The serving maid was still there, but was evidently preparing to leave.

He would have to wait till she had gone and then be sure that she had retired before he ventured into the courtyard. But the night was long, and he had ample time.

Suddenly, faintly, from the nearby hills, he heard a sound that tensed his muscles in fear. It was the bark of a dog—his dog, Bani. There was no mistaking that queer double bark. Never before had he known Bani to leave his sheep. What evil spirit could be possessing him? Was he seeking his master?

Bani barked again. Unmistakably, he was coming closer. Then voices, hushed but excited in the clear air. A boy's voice. Asa's!

"See there! A light! In the stable of the inn! Surely, Jacob, he must be there! Come, Bani, run!"

So they were seeking him—Jacob and Asa. He pressed back hard against the wall, his body as cold as the stone he leaned against. Had Jacob suspected what he was about and come to stop him? With Bani in the lead he would surely be discovered. And what could he say, how explain his presence here? That he had come to see the newborn baby? Even in his fear, he knew that shrewd old Jacob would never accept so unlikely an explanation.

Now he could hear the light tripping of Asa's feet on the courtyard pavement. Perhaps it would be best to act before he was discovered, to step out and rebuke the boy for leaving the flocks. Perhaps by a show of anger he could silence any accusations. He stepped out of the niche, harsh words on his lips.

But Asa and Bani passed him by as though he were no more than one of the cattle munching the hay. Straight to the manger-cradle they ran, with eyes for nothing but its tiny occupant. Softly, hardly breathing, Eliud drew back into the shadows as old Jacob followed close on the heels of the boy.

As he watched, the relief that had swept over him changed to wonder. One after the other, his fellow shepherds emerged from the shadows and stood hesitantly near the manger where the baby slept. On a thick pallet of straw Mary half lay and half sat, surveying the shepherds wonderingly. Joseph, standing nearby, looked at the intruders with irritation.

Behind the group stood Sarah, the serving maid, pausing in

her departure to learn what new event this could be. The little lamp, flickering from a tiny shelflike projection, sent the shadows flying in grotesque shapes along the cavern walls. A rustling of straw among the cattle and the muffled snort of an ox were the only sounds to fill the hushed quiet.

Old Jacob's slow voice trembled through the silence.

"A baby, wrapped in cloths and lying in a manger. That was what the angel said. That was the sign. And here he is—the Savior, the Christ, the Lord!"

Reverently Jacob sank to his knees. One by one the shepherds knelt before the manger and bowed their heads, their rough hands clasped before them.

"Now the time has come!" Jacob's voice was scarcely more than an exultant whisper. "Now the scepter will be restored to Judah and an everlasting kingdom to the house of David. This is the sign, and our waiting is over and done. God the Lord be praised!"

The hush of worship was finally broken when Asa rose to his feet.

"I must go to my uncle," he said, "and tell him the glad news."

"And I," Jacob raised himself slowly with the help of his staff. "I must hurry to my son. He, too, must see the Lord's salvation."

"And my father must know," eagerly spoke another. "He has waited long for this day!"

In greater haste than when they had come, the shepherds departed. Eliud raised a shaking hand to his damp brow. Why had they not seen him—not even his dog? And why had they all come? Of old Jacob he could understand such foolishness. He had long been obsessed by the idea that he would someday see the Christ. But that the other shepherds should so carelessly desert their flocks and now hurry away with no thought of returning to the fields! An evil spirit must surely have possessed them.

But the parents of the newborn baby seemed to have no fear of evil spirits. Mary turned to Joseph with a smile. Slowly, Joseph smiled in response.

"It is true," he said. "The Lord has blessed you most wonderfully—you and the child."

"And you, Joseph. You also." Her eyes followed him gently as he turned away and stooped to pick up his cloak from the pile of straw. Then she turned to the child in the manger and settled him more comfortably in his rough bed.

Sarah, the serving maid, was standing motionless, her wide eyes fastened on the sleeping baby.

"Truly?" she whispered hoarsely. "Have I—these rough hands of mine—helped to bring the Christ into the world? God have mercy on me. How can such a thing be?" and, clasping the cloths she held tightly to her bosom, she ran from the stable.

Mary settled herself wearily on the straw while Joseph spread his travel-stained mantle over her.

"Rest now, Joseph," she said beseechingly. "It is safe here, and you are weary. Soon the dawn will come."

Dazedly, Eliud waited. Was this child actually the King of Israel, the long-awaited Christ—here in a stable? Jacob had spoken of an angel. Could one really have appeared to them that night and told them of this child?

When sleep had smoothed the breathing of the traveling pair, Eliud stole closer to the manger and gazed intently at the child. Certainly, there was nothing unusual about him. His round red face, puckered lips, and tightly closed eyes looked like any ordinary baby's. There was no more glory in that wizened face than there had been in the face of his own short-lived son. Old Jacob must have bewitched them all with his fantasies.

Quietly he stole between the rows of cattle to the entrance of the cavern. All was dark and still in the courtyard. Involuntarily he glanced up at the starry sky. Would he, too, have seen the angel if he had been with the others? Suppose an angel appeared now among those myriad stars? His heart quailed suddenly.

But in the heavens the stars shone remote and undisturbed. With a muttered oath he stooped and unlatched his sandals. If angels were about, let them look the other way. Silent as a snake he began to mount the stairs.

His ear, sharpened by caution, caught a faint rustle from the steps above. He had scarcely time to flatten himself against the wall when a slight figure passed him. The silken rustle and the faint perfume convinced him that this was none other than Naomi, the rich man's daughter. What could she be doing here—and alone? She descended slowly, feeling for each step in the darkness, her hand tightly clutching the railing. At the bottom she paused a moment, then, guided by the light in the far corner, entered the stable.

It was only a second before Eliud turned to follow her. Perhaps she still wore that chain of gold and pearls.

She was stepping daintily across the stone floor, her skirts lifted to avoid the dirt. Now and then she paused to look uneasily about her. As she approached the rays of the lamp, Eliud's eager eyes caught the dull gleam of gold and pearls around her neck. Surely the Lord was with him tonight!

The pious phrase came unbidden to his mind. Irritably he brushed it aside. The Lord had nothing to do with this. After all, he was not doing it for himself. He despised a thief as much as any Israelite. Nor had he ever stolen as much as a farthing from any man. But that trinket around the young girl's neck would easily take Rachel to Alexandria, and pay a worthy physician's fee besides.

It was his only chance. Of late he had been tormented by imagining that he had seen in Rachel's face a fleeting glimpse of returning spirit. But when his eager eyes searched further, he was met by the same heartbreaking, vacant stare. It must be done—and now!

Naomi stood, hands clasped tightly before her, gazing at the child in the manger. It would take but a moment to creep up behind her, strike her with his staff, and tear the chain from her throat. He would not hurt her, only stun her, that she might not cry out and betray him. It would all be done so quietly that none of the sleepers would wake.

But Naomi heard him. She turned and sprang aside with a gasp of fear to see this man with the burning eyes but two feet from her. Then she noticed his clothing and the shepherd's staff in his hand.

"Oh!" she murmured in quick relief. "You are one of the shepherds. How you frightened me! Have you come to see the child? But hush. Do not waken him!" She smiled up at Eliud's strained face, then turned and lightly touched the baby's cheek. A bit wistfully she went on: "I did not know, last night. They could have lodged in my room. The little serving maid told me of it when I could not sleep and asked her to bring me drink. I would have come to see how they fared, but my father forbade me. So I waited till they all slept, and no one knows that I am here!" She smothered a girlish laugh.

Eliud scarcely heard her. His gaze never left her throat. With mounting heartbeat he realized that now, if he would have the necklace, it would no longer suffice merely to stun her. She must not later be able to say who it was had stolen her jewels.

She turned eagerly again to the shepherd. "Tell me truly, did you see the angel? Is this really the Christ? Strange, that on so slender a thread the salvation of Israel should hang!"

The angel again! Would all the world keep telling him of the angel? For him there would be no tidings of joy, but a flaming sword turned against him, a thief and a murderer! He would return to Rachel with the brand of Cain on his brow, but Rachel would be healed. Quickly he transferred his staff to his left hand and, with clammy fingers, reached for his knife.

Naomi, all unconscious, had turned again to the manger. Her thoughtful half-whisper no more disturbed the sleepers than the rustling of hay among the cattle.

"The Christ! The Anointed One! The King of Israel! A king should not lie in a stable! Kings have gold and jewels and ivory palaces!" Her white hands groped for her necklace. With sudden determination she loosed the clasp and drew the jewels caressingly through her fingers.

"Gold and pearls—a king's gift! I will give it to the Christ, because he must lie in a manger while I sleep in a bed. Now, shepherd!" She laughed softly up at Eliud. "Do not look so concerned! My father will know nothing of it. I shall tell him it was lost. He has often rebuked me for my carelessness. So I will give it to the Christ, though indeed it is a beautiful thing, and I love it dearly!"

She held the costly thing high in her hands, where the little lamp shed its full glow upon it. Then she knelt beside the manger, took the sleeping child's hand in hers, and tenderly wrapped the chain about his wrist. Softly she kissed the tiny fingers and rose to go.

"Do not betray me, shepherd! How strangely you stare! But you wish to worship the child alone. I will go! Do not betray me!" With a rustle of silken skirts she brushed past Eliud and sped into the darkness.

Eliud scarcely breathed as he stooped over the manger, carefully raised the child's arm and unwound the chain. One moment he held it exultantly in his hand, then thrust it into his belt and strode out into the night.

Chill dawn was lightening the eastern sky when Eliud reached the sheepfold and threw himself down beside the fire. None of his comrades was asleep. They hailed him with exclamations of joy, and old Jacob at once began to recount the events of the past night.

But Eliud was in no mood for listening. Before Jacob was fairly started, he rudely interrupted.

"Now, Jacob! Do not speak constantly to me of this Christ of yours! Do you think there was never a child born in Bethlehem till now?"

"But, Eliud!" Jacob's old voice quavered indignantly. "The angels sang to us, and . . . "

"Surely, surely!" interrupted Eliud impatiently. "Old men are always seeing visions and dreaming dreams!"

"No, Uncle!" objected Asa. "We all saw the angels and heard their song, not only old Jacob."

"Oh, indeed, indeed!" Eliud sounded exasperated. "You are all dreamers; not a sane man among you. It would have been far wiser to have stayed with the flocks and not leave them to the dangers of the night!"

A sullen silence fell upon the group. Restlessly Eliud stretched out his staff and thrust a wayward bit of brush into the flames.

"Well, then, you skeptic!" grumbled Jacob at last. "If the angels' song and the birth of the Anointed One means nothing to you, perhaps this will. Simeon has learned in the village that Philip of Alexandria, being of David's lineage, is in Bethlehem and is lodging at the inn."

"What are you saying?" The agitated staff was suddenly still.

"Philip of Alexandria, the physician, is in Bethlehem—unless he is already on his way to Jerusalem. Surely, he will not stay longer than to register."

"Simeon, is it true?"

Simeon shrugged. "I am a dreamer and dream dreams. How should I know?"

"Simeon, forgive me! Jacob, I did not mean to be rude. But lately I do not know whether I come or go. Is Philip of Alexandria truly in Bethlehem?"

"So they say." Simeon was somewhat mollified. "With my own eyes I did not see him, of course. But they speak of horses and a chariot of gold, which the innkeeper must be keeping well hidden, for we saw nothing of them when we went to worship the child. But in the town it is said that he is there."

Eliud was already on his feet when Jacob laid a restraining hand on his arm.

"When you come to Bethlehem, Eliud, and have seen the physician, do not fail to go to the stable to see the Christ!"

"That I will, friend Jacob!" answered Eliud, and as he ran, the path to Bethlehem was bright with morning light and hope.

Fires were glowing, maidservants with water jars were hurrying back and forth, stableboys were spreading provender for the animals, and the innkeeper was busily overseeing it all when Eliud once more entered the courtyard.

"Innkeeper!" he cried, not pausing for so much as a breath. "Is Philip of Alexandria still here?"

"Well, now," the innkeeper frowned disapproval. "What does a poor shepherd like you have to do with Philip of Alexandria?"

"He is here then? I must speak with him."

"Now, now!" cried the innkeeper, barring his way up the stairs. "You are an impudent fellow! Philip of Alexandria is but now breaking his fast and will leave thereafter for Jerusalem. He has no time for such as you!"

"But my wife is ill, and I have heard . . . "

"Is your wife the only woman ill in Bethlehem? And can Philip heal them all? Besides, in all your lifetime you cannot earn the fee that the great man exacts."

"But I have money—jewels," protested Eliud desperately. He drew the chain of gold and pearls from his belt and held it up before the astonished innkeeper.

"Where did you get that?" he inquired suspiciously.

"Does it matter to you?" retorted Eliud with a show of anger. "Take the chain to Philip of Alexandria. It shall be his if he will heal my wife."

In a few moments the innkeeper beckoned to him from the top of the stairway.

"You must pardon me for my rudeness," he said as Eliud reached him. They turned into the hallway. "It seems that Philip's daughter lost the chain, and he is very glad that it has been found."

Eliud stopped short. Philip's daughter! Naomi, of course! He was a fool not to have guessed! Cold sweat chilled his body, and he would have turned to run, but the innkeeper was already ushering him through the curtained door of the south rooms.

One of the Ethiopian slaves was removing various colored clay dishes from a small table. The physician, reclining on a cushion nearby, was thoughtfully fingering the necklace.

"Welcome, shepherd!" He looked up with a smile as Eliud entered. "Thrice welcome because you have found my daughter's trinket. She has fretted much this morning over its loss."

Trembling visibly, Eliud could think of no reply. He was dimly aware of the powerful Ethiopian brushing by him with his handful of pottery and leaving the room. The innkeeper, too, had disappeared. Desperately, Eliud wanted to follow them, but his legs were too weak to move.

"My daughter will be most happy when the jewels are returned to her." Philip raised his voice slightly. "Naomi, child, come here!"

"Yes, Father?" Naomi's slender figure appeared in the curtained doorway of an adjoining room.

"See, Naomi, what this honest shepherd restores to you!" He held up the jewels for her to see.

Naomi caught her breath audibly. Her eyes darted to Eliud, and, recognizing him, her face paled in anger.

"Honest, did you say, father? How do you know that this fellow has not stolen the jewels?"

"Well, now!" marveled Philip. "This is surely the height of feminine perversity! Only an hour ago, when I would have informed the guard, you were sure that the chain was lost, not stolen! Come now! Give your thanks to this man who has, with an honest heart, returned your jewels when he might profitably have kept them."

"I thank you, shepherd," said Naomi obediently, but her voice was cold. "What reward had you in mind when you came to my father with the jewels you found?"

"Naomi!" Philip frowned and his voice was sharp. "What evil spirit possesses you? If you cannot thank this man with civility you shall not have the jewels! You shall never again wear them about your throat!"

"I do not want them!" cried Naomi passionately. "The chain was . . . I . . . " she choked and burst into violent sobs. "I could not endure to touch it again!" she flung over her shoulder as she ran from the room.

Philip stared after his daughter in utter amazement. Ruefully he turned to Eliud.

"Bear with my daughter, shepherd! She is weary and overwrought with the long journey from Alexandria. But a reward you shall have! Speak, shepherd! What can I do for you?"

Clumsily, Eliud wiped his damp forehead with his sleeve.

"Sir . . . " He paused to steady his voice. "For two long years my wife has been afflicted with an illness of the mind. Since our firstborn died, she has not smiled, nor scarcely spoken, though she remains gentle and obedient. She has no interest in life or living and would not even eat if I did not urge her. Sir, I have heard that you can heal such sickness."

"Shepherd, the healing belongs to God. But at times he gives me power to interpret his ways. Is your wife in Bethlehem?"

"Scarcely a stone's throw distant."

"Bring her here. Perhaps help may be found for her."

Eliud choked out something by way of reply, then stumbled from the room. At the base of the stairs he ran full tilt into little Leah, who fell sprawling to the ground. One second he knelt to raise her and brush back her tangled hair, then rose to rush on.

At that instant he caught sight of a slender, gray clad figure among the others in the crowded courtyard. She walked hesitantly, yet with a certain purpose, toward the stable. As she passed the still-whimpering Leah, she turned to smile at the child. Eliud saw that it was, indeed, Rachel! Rachel smiling!

"Rachel." He said it gently, not to frighten her.

She turned to him, and her eyes were shining and her lips laughing.

"Here you are, Eliud! Asa came during the night looking for you. He spoke of angels and a wonderful child here in the stable. Have you seen him, Eliud? Let us go together."

She took his limp hand, and they entered the cavern. Mary was alone; Joseph had gone to fetch food for their morning meal. The mother sat with her back against the cold stone wall, holding the child in her arms; and she smiled as they came near.

"Blessed among women," murmured Rachel. "Give joy to a childless mother, and let me hold your son!"

"Yes," said Mary. "He is heavy and tires me. Lay him in the manger again."

With a gracious gesture Rachel stooped and gathered the baby to her breast. Tenderly she held him close.

"See, Eliud, how his tiny fingers curl around mine and will not let me go?" Her voice was low and vibrant, as he had not heard it for many years. "He is so soft and sweet, like our own so long ago, is he not, Eliud?"

He could not answer, dared scarcely breathe, so afraid was he of shattering this dream of his wife's awakening. But she came closer to him, held the baby high, and pressed his fragile fist against Eliud's cheek.

"I have something to tell you, Eliud," she said softly. "The Lord has had mercy and has heard me in my distress. I am with child these three months."

"Rachel?" he could only whisper it hoarsely.

"It is true, Eliud. I did not tell you sooner because I thought surely the child would die. But now I know, as surely as this child's hand clings to mine, so surely will our child live and bring us joy. The Lord has been gracious, Eliud."

Silently Eliud gazed at this wonder of his wife and the child in her arms. A great hope was struggling in his heart, but he dared not let it rise. The despair, the evil he had planned, the guilt and terror he had experienced, had it all been unnecessary? Could this possibly be true? Were his sins being so incredibly rewarded? Was Rachel once more—Rachel?

As they stood together, Joseph entered, picking his way carefully between the cattle, in his hands a steaming bowl of pottage. He eyed them with obvious disapproval, but even his stern features melted before Rachel's smile. She turned to lay the baby in its bed.

"Shepherd, is this your wife?" a voice behind Eliud inquired. Philip of Alexandria stood watching Rachel with grave eyes. Beside him stood Naomi, face swollen and red with weeping.

"My daughter wanted me to see the child," explained Philip. "It is here she lost the chain. But I did not expect to meet you here. Your wife . . . Surely, there is nothing amiss with her?"

"Truly, sir," Eliud's voice trembled with struggling joy and fear. "I do believe the child has worked a miracle in her!"

"Ah, yes!" nodded the physician. "How often I have seen it!

Man worries and troubles himself mightily for a cause which God rights with his little finger!"

He paused and drew from his girdle the chain of gold and pearls.

"It seems your wife has no need of my help, and you have not yet been rewarded. Since my daughter will have nothing to do with this bauble, use it for whatever you will—for your wife and yourself."

Mechanically, Eliud took the chain held out to him. The glowing pearls seemed to burn into his flesh. Slowly he shook his head.

"It is not mine." He looked at Rachel, then at Naomi. And Naomi's sullen face lit up in sudden understanding.

"It is the Christ's," he said, and with reverent step approached the manger.

Joseph stared in wonder. Mary and Rachel smiled at one another across the sleeping baby. But for Eliud, as he knelt and tucked the chain carefully into the little fist, the touch of the tiny hand seemed to hold the gift of a special grace.

(This story is based on the Biblical account given in Luke 2:1-20.)

Breakfast for Matthias

It was gray dawn, and the wet sand was chilly under Caleb's bare feet. He did not really need to be here, but what good reason could there be for lying in bed when one could stand in the fresh sea breeze and listen to the shouts of the fishermen across the water as they brought in their boats? Besides, his grandfather, old Matthias, often told him that he was a great help when the boats came in.

Matthias no longer went out in the boats with the fishermen. He was too old and not strong enough. There was no room in the boats, said the men, for one whose arms could not pull their weight on the oars or whose fingers failed when the nets grew heavy with fish. So Matthias would wait until the boats came in. Then he would help the men sort the fish.

He did good work, for he had a good eye and a steady aim, and the baskets he filled could be counted on to contain fish of uniform size and variety. The fish that were small, or for some other reason not easily marketable, he was allowed to keep. He and Caleb would bear them in triumph up the stony path to the village, where, in the smallest cottage on the farthest edge of the town, Caleb's mother waited to bake them for her family's breakfast.

So they stood there, hand in hand, the old man and the boy, watching the boats come in. The rising sun began to shed a welcome warmth on Caleb's cheeks, but he felt his grandfather's hand tighten in anxiety. For the boats were coming in silently, quietly, with none of the boisterous laughter and exuberant shouting that marked a good catch. Caleb knew, too, what that meant—no shouts, no fish. No breakfast.

One by one the boats reached shore, and the men stepped out, dragging their empty nets up onto the sand. One by one they shook their heads as Caleb and his grandfather approached. There were no fish to sort. One man had caught five small ones. Of these he gave Matthias the two smallest, and Matthias laid them carefully into Caleb's hands.

"Bring these to your mother," he said, "and take care that you do not drop them. I will stay awhile. There will be nets to clean and mend. Perhaps . . . "

He did not finish his sentence. There was not much reason to. Money did not come easily to fishermen, nor was it easily given. But perhaps . . .

With the concentration of a hungry boy whose breakfast depended on his own efforts, Caleb managed to deliver the fish to his mother without mishap. As she cleaned them and laid them on the little fire, Caleb sniffed at the baking loaves beside them.

"Why did you make only five?" he asked. "I could eat them all myself."

"The barley meal is gone," said his mother. "And so is the oil." She lifted the loaves from the fire and placed them on a small white cloth spread on the mat before her.

"Like the widow who fed Elijah," said Caleb. "She had no more meal or oil, but she fed Elijah with what she had, and after that there was always enough."

"I wish there were such an Elijah *I* might feed," answered his mother wearily. "But there are no Elijahs in Israel today and, sometimes I think, no God either." Her voice sank to a low murmur, and Caleb, his attention caught by the sheen of a spider's web in the sunshine in a corner of the doorway, scarcely heard it.

"What did you say, Mother?" If he tapped the edge of the web ever so lightly with his finger, the spider would come dashing out for its own breakfast. But that would hardly be fair, and he withdrew his hand.

"Never mind," said his mother. "It is just that sometimes I wonder what God has in mind for us since your father died."

"But, Mother," Caleb came closer to argue. "He cares for us. You have said so yourself. We have food, and clothing, and . . ."

"And no water," she said, with a little laugh that sounded a bit like a sob. "Go and fetch some now, and when you return the fish will be ready. The jar is by the door."

Carefully avoiding the spider's web, Caleb stepped outside, but just as he was about to lift the jar to his shoulder, a partridge whistled invitingly from a nearby clump of tall grass. There might be little ones about, he knew; so he approached the clump warily. He did not like to frighten them. Slowly, slowly, each movement taking him almost imperceptibly closer, he approached the tall grass. And his patience was rewarded. Instead of a sudden flurry of wings in panic, he watched with delight the mother hen leave her hiding place and, in great dignity, lead her fat little chicks across the path to the shelter of a large rock.

He took one tentative step toward the rock, when he heard his mother calling. He sent an apprehensive glance toward the still empty water jar, but went directly into the house. She was laying the freshly baked fish on the cloth beside the loaves. Then she drew up the corners of the cloth and knotted them securely.

"Take these now to your grandfather," she said. "Two of the loaves and one fish you may have, but do not stop to eat till you have given the rest to your grandfather. Perhaps your own hunger will hurry your feet!"

She laid the neatly tied bundle in his hands and gave him a gentle push on his way. But Caleb did not go.

"There were only five loaves," he said, "and you have given them all to me. What will you eat?"

"I am not hungry. I will eat later. But Matthias is old and must have food or he will sicken and die, and no provider will be left for us. Hurry now, and do not stop to play, or he will hunger and faint in the day's heat."

The sun was hot, but the air was still fresh. Caleb told himself to remember to fill the water jar the first thing after he came back. He held his bundle carefully in both hands as he walked down the stony path to the sea.

But the shore was deserted. The boats had been pulled up high onto the sand, and the nets, instead of being spread wide in the sun, lay in great soggy heaps beside them. Not a man was in sight.

What had happened? Why would all the fishermen, including Matthias, leave so hurriedly that they did not even have time to care for their nets properly? And where had they gone?

Uncertainly, Caleb wandered along the shore. The little shells in the sand at his feet sparkled in the sunshine. He picked up one or two of the largest ones and tucked them into the soft folds of his belt. Occasionally, when he caught sight of a particularly satisfactory flat round stone, he would pick it up and weigh it carefully in his hand. Then he would launch it low into the air and over the lake, watching it skip and skim like a low-flying bird over the quiet water. He was careful, always, to set down his bundle only where the sand was smooth and dry, and only once did he accidentally step on it.

Farther along Caleb glimpsed a group of fishermen. He hurried to join them, but they were hurrying, too, and before he caught up with them they were quite some distance north of the village. Just over the next rise, Caleb knew, the sand and rocks and gullies gave way to a large grassy meadow where he had often played.

And that was where everyone was. Hundreds of people, thousands, perhaps. He had never seen so many! They were sitting or standing quietly in the sun, and it struck him as strange that so many people could be so hushed. One man was speaking. He was sitting on a large rock somewhat apart from the rest. His voice was not loud, but he spoke with a clarity and urgency that made even the children splashing in the shallow shore water subdue their play.

Caleb drew a deep sigh. How would he ever find Matthias in that crowd?

He did not try very hard. He laid his bundle carefully on a rock, away from the edge of the crowd, beneath a clump of oleanders. Then he went down to the water. Some of his friends were there, and he joined them in their play. They were digging a canal in the sand by the water's edge. The breeze had freshened, and it was exciting to guess which wave would finally leap over the intervening sand and fill their canal to its farthest end.

While Caleb played, the voice of the man on the rock seemed to reach out and draw him closer. Then Caleb would stop and listen. God's children should never worry, the man said, because their heavenly Father could care for them just as surely as he cared for the flowers at their feet and the birds soaring above their heads.

Caleb wished his mother could hear. She worried. She did not like to wear old and worn clothing, and she liked to know there was food for the next day waiting on the shelf. He wished she could hear this man tell her not to worry. Caleb never worried. But then, of course, he always had his mother to care for him. And his grandfather.

Matthias *must* be hungry. Caleb started back to the clump of oleanders where he had left the food. He had not realized that he had wandered so far along the water's edge. Finally he found the bundle, but it wasn't until he had picked it up that he realized his hands were still covered with sand. He went back to the water and rinsed them carefully, drying them sketchily on his tunic. Already the sun was high in the sky and hot, and the shade of the oleanders felt cool and refreshing. He opened the bundle and spread the loaves and the fish on the grass beside him. But he did not eat. He really ought to find Matthias first.

Patiently he restored the food to the no longer white cloth and clumsily retied the knots. It wasn't a very neat piece of work, but if he carried it carefully, it would hold the food until he found Matthias. He put the bundle back on the rock, yawned, stretched, settled himself comfortably on the grass with his head on his arm, and fell fast asleep.

The oleanders were casting long shadows over the grass when he awoke. There was noise and confusion all around him. He sat up and reached guiltily for his bundle. It was still there. And he was very hungry.

He got to his feet and looked around. The man had stopped talking, and the people were milling about, apparently not knowing what to do next, yet reluctant to leave. A small group of men stood near the rock where the man had spoken. Suddenly Caleb recognized one of them. It was Andrew, of nearby Bethsaida, who had often fished near their village with Peter and Philip before they became followers of Jesus.

Slowly it became clear to Caleb. The man who had been teaching the people was Jesus himself! He felt an instant's regret. If he had known that, he would have listened more carefully. His mother would want to know what Jesus had said.

He *must* find his grandfather! What would his mother say if Matthias came home faint and exhausted because Caleb had not brought his food? He decided to go to Andrew. Perhaps Andrew had seen Matthias.

Around Jesus all the men seemed to be talking at once. Caleb recognized Peter's big voice. "This is a lonely place, and the hour is late," he said.

Philip joined in: "Send the crowds away to go into the villages and buy food for themselves."

Caleb tugged at Andrew's sleeve. Andrew turned, and his worried face broke into a smile when he recognized Caleb. But he spoke softly, that he might not disturb the discussion.

"Young Caleb! How you have grown! Do you want to see Jesus?"

Caleb shook his head. "No," he said. "I must find Matthias. I have brought food for him, but I cannot find him in this crowd." Caleb lifted his grimy bundle, and with the movement the insecure knots suddenly parted. Had it not been for Andrew's quick hands, Caleb's loaves and fish would have lain scattered on the ground. As the man and boy began to laugh in quick relief, Jesus' voice came to them.

"They need not go away. You give them something to eat."

"It would take at least two hundred denarii to buy enough bread for each of them to get even a little," protested Philip.

Still laughing, holding the soiled cloth and the food in his hand, Andrew turned to Jesus.

"Here is a boy who has five barley loaves and two fish, but what are they among so many?"

"Bring them here to me," said Jesus, and as he took them from Andrew, it seemed to Caleb that the poor soiled cloth gleamed suddenly white and pure, and the crumbled and broken loaves and fish grew fresh and succulent in his hands.

"Make them sit down in groups, about fifty each." As the disciples went among the people, organizing them, Jesus lifted his eyes to heaven, and Caleb bowed his head as he blessed the food. Then he broke the flat loaves Caleb's mother had baked over her small fire that morning, and there was enough that each disciple received a piece, both of the bread and the fish.

Caleb followed Andrew, his eyes wide with wonder. Andrew paused beside one of the groups, broke the bread and fish in his hands—and there was enough that the father of each family in his group received a piece, both of the bread and the fish. And each father gave part of his piece to his wife and children, so that down to the smallest babe, whose mother pressed the softest crumb into the wet little mouth, all had enough to eat. And the fathers held in their hands still more pieces, and looked about them, for none of their families still desired food.

It was then that Caleb saw his grandfather just a few rows away. He was standing and looking about, as if searching for someone to share the food he held in his hand. Caleb shouted and waved.

"Caleb!" called Matthias, as he recognized him. "Have you eaten?"

Dizzy, Caleb remembered that he had not. He made his way through the ranks of people to his grandfather. The old wrinkled face lit up with the smile Caleb loved, and the tired eyes looked strangely young and excited.

"Did you see it?" the old man demanded. "How he fed us all with the few loaves and fishes? Like manna in the wilderness! This is the prophet like Moses—the one who is to come—the Messiah who will set us free! We must make him our king!" He pressed the food into Caleb's hands. "I must go," he said urgently. "There are others who feel as I do. We must make him our king!"

Caleb sat down and began to eat. It was the same coarse barley bread his mother had prepared that morning, and the same fish his grandfather had laid into his hands in the early sunlight. They tasted just as Caleb remembered his mother's barley loaves and fish had always tasted. Caleb ate and was satisfied. Then, because he sensed that his satisfaction lay in something deeper than merely appeased hunger, he rose to return to Jesus.

But Jesus was no longer there. His disciples were there, gathering up the fragments of food that were left over. But Jesus was gone.

Caleb was not the only one looking for Jesus. The quiet talk of the multitude had swelled to an excited roar. Shouts and cries of "Jesus! Our king, Jesus!" and "Let us have a king who can give us bread!" filled the air. The crowd was on its feet and moving. Caleb, all alone and a little frightened in the rush and excitement of the mob, decided it was time to go home.

Andrew caught him just as he reached the edge of the crowd. He pressed into the boy's hand a wicker basket, heavy with remnants of the bread and fish with which he had left home that morning. It was neatly covered with his mother's white cloth.

"Take it to your mother," said Andrew, hurriedly. "Tell her all that has happened, for she needs to know."

This time Caleb did not loiter. He carried the heaped basket carefully over the rocks and across the sand and up the hill to the village.

His mother was sitting at her loom when he reached home, and he thought he had never seen her look so weary. She did not turn to greet him. Her hands worked slowly, monotonously, at the loom, but there was no yarn in the shuttle.

"Why do you come back?" she asked, and something in her voice frightened Caleb. "Here there is no food, no oil, no meal, no Elijah. You must go out and beg for food. Here you will starve."

"Mother"; Caleb set his basket down carefully and went to her. "See, Mother."

"And there is no water," went on that toneless voice. "Twice I have tried to lift the jar to go to the well, and twice I have failed. There is no strength left in me. My son does not fetch water; my father does not bring food. I sit at the loom and weave and there is no yarn. No yarn, no hope, no God!"

Desperately, Caleb caught at those weary, monotonously busy hands and stopped them. "Mother, see, I have food," he urged; and when she finally turned to him, he ran to get the basket. He brought it to her and lifted the cloth, only to see her slip from her stool and fall limply to the floor.

Caleb screamed, "Mother! Mother!" And from the doorway came the most welcome sound he had ever heard, Matthias' voice.

"What is it?" he cried. "Here, Caleb, get some water, quickly!" Caleb caught up the empty water jar and ran to the nearby well.

When he returned, his mother was sitting up, with Matthias at her side, rubbing her hands. Caleb brought her water, and she smiled tremulously as she drank a little of it.Then she turned to the basket.

"Is it—is it bread?"

"Yes, Mother! And fish! See? From Jesus and Andrew!" And while she ate of the food, child and grandfather told her the story of the wonderful loaves and fish.

"From *my* bread?" she said wonderingly. "From the fish *I* baked? And I thought it would not be enough for the three of us!" She began to laugh, a little wildly, but Caleb was relieved to see the color returning to her face and a new sparkle in her eyes.

"He is a miracle-worker!" agreed Matthias. "Like Moses and Elijah—a man who could care for us like Moses and Elijah—who could lead us to victory over those abominable Romans!" He was growing more and more excited, but suddenly checked himself. "But it is very strange. When we looked for him to proclaim him king, he was gone!"

"Gone?"

Matthias nodded. "Later we saw his disciples leave by boat, but he was not with them. He must have gone off to the mountain by himself. But it is strange that no one saw him go."

"Maybe he didn't want them to," said Caleb. "Maybe he doesn't want to be a king."

Matthias frowned.

"Not want to be king? But then why the miracle? We were all hungry, to be sure, but none of us would have starved before we could reach our homes, even as far as Bethsaida. Why would he at this time, near Passover, feed us in the wilderness, like Moses, if he does not want us to believe that he *is* the prophet like Moses, whom God promised? And how can he lead us to our final victory unless he proclaims himself? I simply do not understand it!"

"Perhaps," said Caleb's mother slowly, "it is not necessary to understand. Perhaps we need only accept." She drew the white cloth carefully over the remaining fragments in the basket. "And this I accept from him—this great gift—greater than any multiplying of loaves and fishes." Something of her old vigor came back into her voice as she spoke, and Caleb's heart lightened. "I accept from him God's love, for that is what he came to show. My five little loaves, those two pitifully small fish—and he fed thousands of people with them? I don't understand it, but I believe it. So I give in return my faith. Never again will I doubt God's love. Jesus has proved it. And for now that is enough."

"There are those," said Matthias thoughtfully, "who are planning to find him tomorrow and insist that he become our king. I had thought to go with them. But no, I will not. As you say, for now this is enough." And he helped her lift the basket to the shelf for safekeeping against the next day's breakfast.

(This story is based on the Biblical account as given in John 6:1-15.)

Aryth

"Talitha cumi!"

She had used the greeting every morning since her little daughter had been old enough to want to lie lazily in bed late into the day. Yet this morning she hesitated. The girl lay there breathing lightly and peacefully, her face no longer flushed with wild fever, nor ivory with the pallor of death. She used her name instead.

"Come, Aryth, it is time to get up."

The girl stirred, but did not awake. She needs sleep, thought Arusha. Why wake her at all? But Jairus had insisted that the child's routine be kept as regular as before, and, as usual when the matter came up, Arusha felt small qualms of guilt at her inability to measure up to Jairus' standards of efficiency. Ah, well, she thought, I can at least wake her on schedule.

"Aryth!" she said again, and touched her lightly on the cheek.

Aryth woke easily then, her eyes bright with health and anticipation. Yet she lay in bed a little and stretched her young limbs luxuriously.

"Is the Rabbi here again?"

"No. He is gone."

"Was I sick, Mother?"

"Yes. Very sick."

"I was sleeping so hard when he woke me. He seemed to call to me from a long way off. I had slept so long!"

"Did you dream?" She should not have asked.

Aryth shook her head. A slight frown of concentration wrinkled her delicate brows. "No. I do not think so. It was different. It felt good," she finished, a little lamely. "Mother, why did the Rabbi come to wake me? And why did the men with him look so surprised when I got up? It was very strange to see them all here in the room."

"Your father asked the Rabbi to come, and he brought his friends. Now you must get up and wash. I have little cakes and some fruit for your breakfast."

"Did the Rabbi make me better?"

"Yes."

"Is he a doctor, like Jonas bar Asa?"

"He is a healer. Jonas could do no more to help you, so your father called the Rabbi. He healed you."

Aryth frowned. "He did not have to come. I was only sleeping. I would have waked by myself."

"No," said her mother. "You would not have. Now come and eat; it is time."

Aryth threw off the light cover and sat up. "Then may I go out and play? It seems such a long time."

Arusha hesitated. She looked at the bright eyes and rosy cheeks, remembering yesterday's cold stillness, and wondered what was the right thing to say.

"You may go with me to the market later. But I do not think you should play with your friends yet. You have been very sick."

Aryth loved going to the market. It was full of fascinating things—colorful woven baskets, brightly painted pottery, dates and figs and nuts and luscious baked sweets, some of which her mother always bought for her. Lambs and goats bleated mournfully in one corner, and above their clamor the chatter of buying and selling surrounded them like the dust from continually moving feet. Men with pigeons in small cages slung over their shoulders on bouncing poles made their way awkwardly through the crowds, calling out their wares. Rows and rows of ground spices were heaped on trays like small gay sand piles—bright red and orange and brown and yellow—and when the market woman measured out a little into her mother's container, Aryth always sneezed. Sometimes a merchant from the east would be selling brilliantly colored silks, silks Aryth had never dared to touch, but from which, her mother assured her, she would one day be allowed to select a length for her wedding. And always they would meet friends and stop to talk and laugh above the din, comparing bargains and deploring the high prices.

But today something was different. They started happily enough, with Aryth chattering her delight at being once more out in the dusty streets, the sunlight, and fresh air. Yet before long her exuberance began to diminish, and she looked about her uneasily. For everywhere they went, people were staring at them—not only strangers, but the neighbors they had known and been friendly with for years, and some whom they knew only by sight. They all came out of their walled houses as if to look at some curiously strange thing passing by. Neighborhood gossips stopped speaking at their approach; their eyes followed them in awe. Finally, when one of Aryth's own friends responded to her wave of greeting by hurrying into the house, Aryth turned to her mother in bewilderment.

"Mother . . . "

"It does not matter, dear." Her mother clasped her hand more tightly and hurried on. "They are only surprised to see you up and about so soon. You were very ill, you know."

But they did not linger long at the market. After a few purchases they turned back, and Aryth felt that her mother shared her relief when the walls of their own little courtyard closed around them.

It was two days before Aryth ventured out again. She had been playing alone in the courtyard when she heard children outside and knew they were her friends. "Perhaps they've come to see me," she thought. "By now they know I'm better." And she slipped through the courtyard gate.

The voices stopped promptly. They stood in an uneasy little

semicircle in the street before her—Judith and Hannah and Ruth—and said nothing.

"Hello!" said Aryth.

"Hello!" they answered in a diffident chorus. They looked embarrassed.

"I'm better now," said Aryth brightly. "We can play together again. Where are you going?"

They looked at each other and giggled. "Oh, nowhere," said Judith at last. "Just walking around." They giggled again.

"Well, let's play tag," said Aryth, her brightness growing more determined. "I can run as fast as you, now. You're it!"

She reached out to touch Hannah, but Hannah drew back in alarm. Judith giggled again, but Ruth looked positively frightened.

"What is it?" cried Aryth. "Why are you afraid of me? I'm not sick any more!"

The three looked at each other again, this time too unnerved even to giggle. Finally Judith blurted out: "You were not just sick, you know. You were dead!"

Shocked, Aryth stood frozen, hand outstretched, her face almost as pale as it had once been in death.

"That is nonsense!" she cried. "I was sleeping. I was sick and sleeping, and the Rabbi came and woke me!"

Judith shook her head. "No," she said. "My mother was there, and so was Ruth's. They had started the flutes and the wailing before the Rabbi came. They all knew you were dead!"

"There were no flutes and wailing when I woke up!" protested Aryth desperately. "It was quiet, and only the Rabbi and his three friends were there."

"That's because he put them all out. *He* thought you were just sleeping, too. But everybody knew. They laughed at him. They *knew* you were dead!"

"Then how could he wake me?" demanded Aryth. "No one ever wakes from the dead." The enormity of what must have happened to her left her suddenly gasping. She turned with a wild sob and rushed blindly through the courtyard gate to find her mother.

"You should have told her!" said Jairus harshly.

From her couch Arusha nodded miserably. "I was afraid. I thought it would frighten her, and she would withdraw from me. She was so bright and happy—so full of life—I could not tell her!"

"I should have told her myself," he muttered, pacing restlessly up and down. "After all, I begged him to come. If only that woman hadn't delayed us!"

"What woman?"

"Ah, I didn't even tell you! He was coming with me, and I was trying to hurry him through the crowd before it would be too late, but they pressed and thronged around him and we made little headway. Then this woman—she had been unclean for years—came behind him and touched his robe and was healed. But he knew what had happened and insisted on finding out who had touched him before he would move on. In that crowd! But she finally confessed; I suppose it was something he felt she needed to do. He blessed her and sent her off. It was then that I saw Isaac approaching, and I knew that you had sent him and that it was too late. So I turned to go—why bother the Rabbi any further—but he caught my arm and told me to keep on believing. And somehow I did. Then the crowd cleared away. I think his disciples made a path for us, and we came, as you know. It was not too late—not for him. But for Aryth . . . How much better it would have been for her if he had come before . . . " His voice trailed away.

"She was here today," said Arusha.

"Who?" He stopped short before her.

"That woman—the one he healed. Her name is Neria. She has no money. She has been unclean so long, no one will give her work. I told her to come back tomorrow. She can help me with the cleaning and cooking."

"But you have help. What about Silah?"

Arusha shrugged. "Silah left today. She will work for Jonas bar Asa's wife. She said, working here . . . people ask her too many questions. I did not know she had delayed you, and that was why you came so late."

"Silah had nothing to do with the delay."

"No, no, of course not! I meant Neria!"

"Why did she come to you?"

"I don't really know. Perhaps she heard that Silah was leaving."

"And she would have heard why. Did she see Aryth?"

"No."

"Did she talk about Aryth?"

"No."

"But she did speak of her own healing."

"Yes."

"Obviously she felt that since Jesus had helped us both, we would feel obliged to take her in."

Arusha shook her head stubbornly. "No. You are wrong. It was only when I asked how it was that so strong and healthy a woman should lack work that she told me her story. I don't believe she even knows about Aryth."

"That is most unlikely." He frowned. "She must not work here."

"But why not? I need help, and she needs work. She is strong and capable."

"And talkative. She would be a constant reminder to Aryth of what she must forget."

It was not often that Arusha set her will against her husband's, yet now she firmed her chin and raised her head.

"She is *not* talkative. She has spent many years alone and disgraced. She spoke with great reluctance, fearing that I, too, would refuse her. If I tell her not to speak of Jesus, of how he helped her and Aryth, she will remain silent. Of that I am sure. We owe much to the Rabbi. How can we repay it if not through one who needs *our* help?"

Jairus sighed. "I am glad you do not argue with me often. You are forever in the right! But you must see that she understands completely. One wrong word to Aryth and she must leave."

"She will understand."

Jairus resumed his restless pacing. "It is unthinkable!" he muttered. "How could so great a blessing for us turn into such a horror for the child?"

"We thought only of ourselves," said Arusha bitterly. "We could not bear to lose her. And now she is unhappy. We were selfish. We should have left her with God!"

"It will pass!" said Jairus sharply. "People will become accustomed to her. They will forget within a month."

They did not forget. Several times Aryth ventured out to find her friends and share the old companionship, but each time she returned within a few minutes, lonely, half afraid, miserable. Her mother invited children to the house, giving them sweets and fruits, but when, sensing their restraint, she left them to play alone with Aryth in the courtyard, they soon disappeared.

They spent much time together, mother and daughter. Arusha was delighted at Aryth's new-found interest in learning to cook, in cleaning, in dainty embroideries—until one day she saw a tear splash down onto the linen in Aryth's hands. Arusha dropped her own sewing and took the child into her arms.

"Oh, my dear!" she mourned. "You are so lonely! But it will be better. Your friends will come back. Just give them time!" But Aryth only shook her head numbly and dashed the tears from her eyes.

"It was so wonderful," the mother sighed, smoothing her daughter's hair. "We were so happy when the Rabbi woke you. Surely, Aryth, you must be a little happy, too, that you are still with us—that he woke you?"

"No, I am not," said Aryth flatly. "He should have left me sleeping!" And she pushed herself almost angrily out of her mother's arms.

They went together, mother and daughter, to the lake shore, where Aryth loved to play. They went during the heat of the day, when few others were likely to be there, and for a time Aryth played contentedly enough in the sparkling shallows among the deserted boats. She wandered up the shore, collecting pebbles from the glistening sand, until she was almost out of sight behind a small hillock that extended nearly to the water's edge.

Arusha, seated under the scant shade of a flat-topped acacia became uneasy and debated whether to call her back. She was gathering her loose-flowing robes about her, ready to rise when she heard Aryth scream. Startled, she sprang to her feet. Aryth was running, and after her from behind the hillock, his whole being concentrated on the heavy stick in his hands with which he hobbled along, the crippled figure of a man. Arusha ran to meet them. She clasped the frantic child in her arms just as the man was about to reach her. Seeing Arusha, he stopped short. He leaned on his stick, panting heavily.

"Forgive me, lady!" he gasped. "I—I meant no harm. I only wanted to touch the blessed child. Perhaps it would have helped me." He stood there, humble, abject, distressed, grotesque, yet reaching out a trembling hand toward Aryth. Arusha dashed his hand aside and thrust the child behind her.

"Stop!" she cried, and was shocked at the shrillness of her own voice. "Leave my child alone! What have you to do with her, you miserable wretch? Go away, at once!"

But he stood there stubbornly, hopelessly, his eyes pleading, and Arusha had no choice but to grasp Aryth by the arm and run with her up the pebbly beach into the shelter of the town. Once she looked back. He was still standing there, leaning on his staff, dejected, following with his eyes his vanishing hope, and her heart constricted in sudden remorse over the callousness of her rebuff. Yet how could she have done otherwise? She strangled a sob in her own throat as she led the weeping child through the streets toward the haven of home.

That night when Aryth was asleep they made their decision. They would leave Capernaum and, they hoped, all those who knew of the miracle. Jairus, by trade a buyer and seller of land, knew of a home in a small village to the south among the hills, whose owner had died and whose heirs wished to sell. Though the town was small, it was growing, and Jairus felt he would have no great difficulty setting up his business there. They left within the week. The village was called Nain.

The new house was large, more than adequate to their needs, and more costly than Jairus might have wished. But a flower-banked courtyard, larger than most, set it well back from the noisy street, and in one corner along the wall was a small room with its own door into the street, where Jairus set up his office. Here they could be as isolated as they wished, and for a time they wished it very much indeed.

The first weeks were busy ones. The three women—Neria had come with them—were busy putting the house in order, and Jairus was fully occupied in town making the contacts he needed to establish his business.

Friendly neighbor women came to call, and Arusha gave them cakes and a little wine. But Aryth hid in her room, and Arusha did not press her. It soon became apparent that, even here among strangers, Aryth's fears were not diminishing. Lonely and listless, she sat idly in her room or in the garden, moving to some purpose only when Arusha assigned her household chores or urged her to a game they could play together.

One morning Aryth was helping Neria scrub the flagstones near the courtyard entrance when a young man suddenly appeared at the open gate.

"You have a lovely garden," he said pleasantly, "but those roses need pruning badly; and if you do not cut back that vine, you will get no grapes next harvest." Unhesitatingly, he stepped down the walk and began examining the vine that twined over its arched frame near the house.

Neria sprang to her feet and belatedly swung shut the courtyard gate.

"Who are you?" she demanded, "and by what right do you walk into our garden so . . . so . . . "

"Boldly?" he suggested and laughed. "I am sorry! You see, I used to work here, before—well, quite some time ago. And I came to see if the new owner might need a gardener—a very good gardener who loves this garden as though it were his own. My name is Amos," he added, almost as an afterthought.

"I will ask my mistress," said Neria, and walked past him into the house. Aryth sprang to her feet in haste to follow, but the young man was thoughtlessly blocking her way.

"Have you ever seen a lovelier flower?" he asked, crouching before a proud, snow-white lily on a tall stem. "I planted it here several months ago. This must be its first bloom. It was dead, you know. It looked like a dry, dead onion. And now it is alive with beauty—like something raised from the dead."

Startled, Aryth shrank away from him. But he was not looking at her; in fact, he had spoken the words so softly and so intimately to himself that she was not sure she had heard them correctly.

"It will die again," she heard herself saying, rather curtly.

"Yes," he nodded. "Yes, it will fade and die again. But now it enjoys the light of the sun and the warm summer air and the clear blue sky. Also it needs water. Bring me that container over there." He pointed to where a shabby, dirt-encrusted bowl lay neglected under a bush by the wall. She ran to pick it up.

"There is no water in it," she said. "I will get some." She stepped inside the door and dipped a little water from a jar into the bowl and brought it out to him again. She was not even aware that her mother, coming at Neria's bidding, had seen her and had stopped short in wonder.

Fascinated, Aryth watched as he let the water drip slowly around the base of the flower, directing it with his strong, skillful hand.

"God provides the flowers with sun and air," he said, "but when he does not send rain, man must provide it to keep them alive."

"Are they glad to be alive?" Aryth's question was a hesitant whisper.

He stared at her in astonishment. "Look at them!" he exclaimed. "Could there be such beauty if they had no joy in life? They love life just as we do. Once you have lost it, you know how precious life can be." He had turned from her, and his voice once more took on that low, intimate tone that seemed to speak to something within himself, rather than to her. And again she could not quite be sure of what she had heard.

"You say strange things," said Aryth.

"Do I?" He smiled at her. "You are rather strange yourself, you know. Imagine a child your age wondering if flowers are glad to be alive! All God's children are glad to be alive! Everything loves life!" He spread his arms wide as if to encircle the whole world, though here it was bounded by the stone walls of the courtyard.

"Not if you've once been dead," said Aryth distinctly.

A sudden light leaped into his eyes. "What did you say?"

"I was dead once," said Aryth, and because it was the first time she had spoken the words, they came out harshly.

"Ah!" It was like a long sigh. He seated himself flat on the flagstone walk and turned toward her. "Tell me, do you know Jesus?"

She nodded. "The Rabbi from Nazareth."

"Ah!" again. "Tell me what you know about him."

Aryth shrugged. "It was nothing," she said. "I was sick and sleeping and he woke me. No . . ." Her young voice became harsh again. "I will no longer speak of it so. I was dead, and he raised me!"

"You do not like to speak of it?"

She shook her head. "It is the first time I have said it to anyone!"

"But why? Are you not glad?"

"I was, at first. But then . . . " She closed her eyes, and the loneliness and fear swept over her again and tautened and pinched her pale face.

"I know," he said gravely. "It is too great a thing to live with."

She began to wail. "I should not have told you! Now everyone will know, and we shall have to go away."

"Quiet, quiet!" He reached out his strong hand and drew her down beside him. "No one shall know, I promise you. It will be our secret. Stop crying, and I will tell you about myself, and then you will know you can trust me."

He waited till she had calmed herself. And when he spoke, the light in his eyes seemed to irradiate his whole being.

"How horrible!" exclaimed Aryth.

"Yes," he agreed. "It was horrible. Like waking into a nightmare—until I saw Jesus' face. Then the horror was gone. After that it was only joy. And the joy has been with me ever since." He smiled down into her attentive face.

"I was sick like you. And I was sleeping, I thought later, like you. Then I woke up. I had the feeling that there had been a great noise and wailing, but now all was quiet and I heard only his voice telling me to get up. So I opened my eyes, and I was on a bier just outside the village gates. There were tight cloths wrapped around me so that I had to struggle to sit up. And crowds of people were all staring at me and waiting, and my mother was crying."

"At least I woke up in my own bed," she said thoughtfully, and then surprised herself with a little giggle.

He laughed with her. "Yes, for you that was better. But perhaps, could it be you missed something of the joy, not knowing the horror that came before?"

"Perhaps."

"But weren't you glad at all to come back?"

"Oh, yes!" she said. "I was glad at first. I had been very sick and I had slept so well, and I felt so good when he woke me. But then, later . . . What do you do when people want to touch you?"

He threw back his head and laughed. "I stretch out my arms," he said, stretching them out once more, drawing her into the circle of his joy,"and give them an enormous hug! It does them no good, but they think it might, and their hearts are lifted. And who knows?" He shrugged his shoulders. "Perhaps the love God has so richly shown me overflows a little into them through me. At least it does me no harm, and they go away smiling."

"It frightened me," said Aryth soberly. "People stared at me wherever I went, and my friends ran away. Once a crippled beggar chased me down the beach."

"Ah, yes, I see! That would frighten a little girl. Strange that Jesus would not have foreseen . . . "

"I think he did," interrupted Aryth. "I remember his telling them all—my father and mother and his three friends—not to tell anyone. I wondered why, but then mother brought me food, and I was so hungry I forgot everything else." They laughed together again.

"And since then you have been hiding?"

"Yes. People frightened me. That is why we came here, where no one knows. Except you."

"So your joy in the life God restored to you was destroyed by thoughtless men," he said musingly. "The world is no better the second time you come into it."

"But I thought you loved life?" She sounded disappointed.

"I do. I do! But I also know it is not perfect. Now, what can we do to make it more perfect for you?"

"It already seems better," she said shyly.

He laughed again, and she smiled.

"Good! Good! Now you need to get more sunshine on those pale cheeks. I know. You shall be my assistant here in the garden. We will make it bloom as no garden ever has before. We will tear out all those ugly weeds, like the ugly little fears in your heart; we will water it with love and laughter and, before you know it, you will be as fresh and blooming as any rose or lily in God's good world."

"God grant it!" said Arusha, behind them.

Amos sprang to his feet. A slight flush of embarrassment covered his face. "Your pardon, lady! I am constantly talking too much before I have good grounds for what I say!"

Arusha smiled and shook her head. "It is I who should beg your pardon for listening when you did not know. Is it true? Were you once like Aryth, and the Rabbi woke you?"

"I was dead, my lady, dead, and he raised me," said Amos, but there was neither arrogance nor impertinence in his voice. "It is not so terrible a thought when you give it body in plain words."

Arusha flushed and bit her lip. "You are right," she said. "It seemed good at first not to speak of it, not to frighten the child. Later we realized how great a mistake we had made. But by then it became more and more difficult to put into words." Aryth had risen to stand beside here, and Arusha put her arm about her daughter's slender shoulders. "Perhaps we could not face the responsibility of so great a gift." She smiled down at Aryth, but there were tears in her eyes.

"That is all in the past," said Amos briskly. "Tomorrow may I come and work in your garden?"

"You may work in my garden, and you may talk to my daughter—and God give you grace to make both bloom and flourish!"

Amos nodded. "I shall not betray your trust," he said.

Jairus was a bit more hardheaded. He inquired in the village about the young man, Amos. He came of respectable family, but his father had died when he was quite young, and since boyhood he had worked in the gardens of those few families in the town who were wealthy enough to employ a gardener. He was well spoken of and well liked, "even without the miracle," as nearly every recommendation concluded.

After a week's work Amos stood with Aryth surveying the garden and shook his head. He frowned. "It is not enough, Aryth," he said. "You and I alone can never pluck all these evil weeds out of this beautiful garden. We must have help."

"No!" said Aryth, shrinking instinctively.

"Yes," he said soberly. "You can see for yourself." He waved his arm at the radiant blossoms among which scarcely a weed dared lift its head. "We cannot possibly do it alone. We must have help."

She said nothing, and he smiled down at the panic in her eyes.

"Trust me, Aryth," he said kindly. "There will be no unpleasantness for you. But you do realize, don't you, there must be others besides me?"

She nodded mutely, and he was satisfied.

Next morning he brought with him a pink-cheeked, merry-eyed young girl of about Aryth's age.

"My cousin Rea," he said to Aryth. "She knows nothing whatever about gardening, and you must teach her." He set them to work pinching the buds off the chrysanthemums in the corner while he worked with the vines near the house, and soon he was smiling to himself at the chatter and giggles that broke out like birdsong from the far corner of the garden.

Two years later they were married. Jairus, as all fathers do, protested that she was too young. Arusha, as all mothers do, pointed out that young girls Aryth's age were either about to be married or wishing they were. And there was about Arusha an air of suppressed excitement that made Jairus wonder. But, of course, it was natural that a mother should be excited about her daughter's wedding.

Certainly he had no objections. They had all grown fond of Amos, with his wholesome good sense and sunny cheerfulness. And Jairus, finding him also of a quick intelligence, had soon lured him away from the garden and into his office, where he became an invaluable aid and would soon become a worthy successor to Jairus' business. All was well, and Jairus was content.

The young couple went to live with Amos' mother, a kindly, pleasant soul, whom Aryth came to love. The two mothers grew fond of each other, visited often, and when, after a few months, the announcement was made that they would, in due course, become grandmothers, the bond between them practically reached the dimensions of a conspiracy. At least, so Jairus felt. He would come upon them in the garden, bent over their delicate sewing, chattering and laughing; but at his appearance, or that of Amos or even Aryth, they would suddenly fall silent, then begin to talk about the weather or what sort of stitch would best befit the tiny garments they were making. It puzzled him, but not too seriously. Women were like that, he shrugged, and went off about his business.

He was greatly astonished when Arusha began to make plans

for attending the feast in Jerusalem at Passover, for Aryth's child was to be born shortly thereafter.

"Surely," he said, "you want to be here with Aryth when her time comes!"

"Aryth is young and strong," returned Arusha. "It will do her good to make the journey."

"You expect to take Aryth along?" He could hardly believe it.

"Why not? She wants to go. She feels a deep gratitude, now, for her life, and would like to make a thank offering in Jerusalem." Arusha spoke with a rising excitement that somehow disturbed him. "It will not harm her," she went on. "Surely, now nothing can harm her!" This last came breathlessly and so softly that Jairus was not sure he had heard it.

"Do not take God's blessings for granted!" he said sharply. "We have no promise that nothing can harm her!"

"The Rabbi would not have wakened her except for a long and happy life." she insisted; and since, within himself, Jairus felt much the same, he made no reply.

"Then while we are in Judea, after the feast, we can go to Bethlehem," Arusha added, too casually.

Jairus stared. "What possesses you?" he demanded at last. "Why in heaven's name should you want to go to Bethlehem?"

"I have cousins there," said Arusha with dignity, but her color was rising. "And I think it's time that Aryth should become more aware of her heritage. Did you know," and here she could no longer hide her excitement, "that Amos, too, is of David's line? Like Aryth, through his mother. These two children of David—surely they should know something of David's town?"

"But not now! You are putting Aryth's very life in danger, and her child's, too, with all these plans of travel and visiting! She should remain quietly at home and leave sacrifices and cousins till after the child is born. I will speak to her and Amos. This must not be!"

"She will come to no harm!" repeated Arusha stubbornly. She clutched at his arm to detain him. "Surely," she said, with a sort of desperation in her voice, "you must see that it is very important that—that their son should be born in Bethlehem!"

Slowly her meaning came clear to him, and he could only stare, aghast.

"Is it so incredible?" she went on urgently. "The boy, born of two people brought back from the dead, is it not logical that he could live forever? The prophet says: 'Of his kingdom there shall be no end'; and if Aryth's son is indeed the one for whom we have waited so long, do we have any right to stand in the way of the prophecies? Aryth must go to Bethlehem, and as soon as possible!"

"I think," said Jairus, drawing in his breath slowly, "that you are completely mad!" But his voice did not carry the conviction of his words. She pounced on his uncertainty.

"But you can see it might be so!" she insisted.

"Do Aryth and Amos believe this nonsense?" he asked heavily.

Arusha shook her head. "I have not spoken to them of it," she confessed. "Only his mother and I—we talk of it constantly. But we thought it best not to excite Aryth. She will realize soon enough. Or . . . or do you think she ought to be told?"

"Absolutely not!" He turned on her almost threateningly. "Arusha, you must promise me you will speak to no one about this—this—inconceivable idea of yours!"

Arusha did not answer. She bit her lip and frowned.

"That is not an unreasonable request," he pointed out. "If you are right, God will reveal it in his own time. If you are wrong, you could do great harm to Aryth by arousing in her such unlikely expectation."

So Arusha promised, and it was well that she did, for within the week Aryth's child was born, dead. It would have been a daughter, had it lived.

It was a grievous disappointment. Jairus felt his heart wrung when Aryth said wistfully: "If only the Rabbi who raised me could have been here!" And Amos nodded his agreement. But their depression was short lived. They were young; such experiences were not uncommon; Aryth would soon regain her health and they would look forward to other children as time went by.

It was the two grandmothers who really roused Jairus' sympathy. He watched them as they laid away the tiny garments they had so lovingly stitched, saying, as disappointed grandmothers were expected to say, that these things happen, and, God willing, there would be more children, healthy ones, and the clothing would yet be useful. But the sorrow and bewilderment in Arusha's eyes were such that Jairus felt no triumph in his better judgment.

"I cannot understand it!" she would say over and over when they were alone. "Why should God have allowed the Rabbi to raise them both if not for some such great purpose? And was it not God's doing that they should meet and marry and produce this child? It should surely have been at least a superior child, but now nothing! It is unreasonable!"

"God's ways have never been reasonable," Jairus pointed out mildly.

"That is little comfort!" she retorted angrily. "When we see the Rabbi again, I shall ask him to his face, What is the purpose in all this? Does not God's direction *lead* somewhere?"

"Perhaps we will see him at the feast," soothed Jairus. "He is a great teacher as well as healer. Perhaps he can tell us God's reasoning in this matter."

But when they arrived in Jerusalem—late for the feast because they had hesitated to leave Aryth—they heard that the Rabbi Jesus from Nazareth had been arrested, and that day crucified, because he had claimed to be the Christ, the King.

They were together again by the sea, mother and daughter. Jairus and Amos had heard of property they wished to survey near Capernaum, and, feeling that the distraction of travel would be good for them, the two women had accompanied them. But it was for Arusha, the bereaved grandmother, rather than Aryth, the bereaved mother, that Jairus felt concern.

Aryth had fully recovered her good spirits, and, beyond a

certain lassitude, her health also. Perhaps she was more thoughtful and understanding, but her joy in life—"given me a third time, when I met Amos!"—was undiminished. Memories of the difficult days after her resurrection all but vanished in her pleasure at being once more on the shores of the sea where she had played happily as a child.

Now she sat sedately under an acacia tree with her mother and watched children playing among the boats and in the shallows. She had never held a living child of her own in her arms, and there was a bit of wistfulness in her watching that suddenly dissolved Arusha into a flood of tears.

"Mother, what is it?" cried Aryth, alarmed.

Arusha shook her head and dashed away the tears. She tried to speak, but sobs choked her. It was not until Aryth took her in her arms and held her close, as a mother would her child, that she regained her self-control.

"Forgive me!" she murmured, wiping her eyes. "It was the children, the beautiful children, and the son you should have had."

"It was a girl, Mother," said Aryth, bewildered.

"But it should have been a son! Aryth, don't you see?"Arusha let her eyes wander over the sparkling blue of the sea and the dark, bobbing fishermen's boats pulled up to the shore, and gave a great sigh. "I promised your father not to speak to you of this, but now it cannot matter. Have you never thought that God had some great purpose in mind when he gave you back your life? And Amos, too?"

"Only to show his great love and compassion for human suffering," said Aryth, slowly. "And perhaps to remind us that there will be another life after death—the Resurrection at the end of time. Is that not enough?"

"And why did he bring you and Amos together?" persisted Arusha.

"Because," said Aryth softly, "Amos was the only one who could lift the nightmare and bring me joy in my new life!"

"But there was more!" cried Arusha, trying to check the

shrillness in her voice. "Surely there was more! Two people, once dead but miraculously brought back to life—why should not those two people produce a child, an unusual child, one who should live forever?"

"Mother!" Aryth's face paled.

"Surely you must have thought of that, you and Amos!" cried Arusha desperately. "You are both of David's line. And a child was to be born of David 'whose kingdom should have no end.' Was it not logical? That your child should be the one, the Christ? I had even planned to take you to Bethlehem, that the child would have been born there! But now . . . " Again the tears began to flow, and she turned her face away.

"Oh, Mother!" Aryth pressed her cheek affectionately against her mother's shoulder, and felt her breath caught between a laugh and a sob. "Surely, no grandmother ever expected so much from her first grandchild! But it would have been better if you had spoken of it, because Amos and I had long ago decided that it must be the Rabbi who raised us, Jesus of Nazareth, who was the Christ. And Neria, too."

"Neria?"

"Yes. I found her crying one day shortly after you had returned from Jerusalem with the news that Jesus had been crucified. I insisted on knowing why, so she told me her story, although you had forbidden her to do so. But by then it did not matter."

"But why should Neria have thought *Jesus* was the Christ? There have been healers before."

"It was his insistence that she reveal herself, a shamed, penniless woman, at a time when an obviously more wealthy and influential man was urging him to come heal his daughter before it was too late. She said: 'I felt he was telling me that the healing of my body was not nearly as important as knowing he was my Lord.' Now he is dead, and she is disappointed, too, like the rest of us. All our hopes are destroyed."

Arusha dabbed the tears from her cheek. "We are a pair of foolish women!" she declared. "But I suppose every generation since the last prophet has been hoping to find the Christ in its midst. And we forget those other prophecies that do not fit our little schemes. 'He shall suddenly appear in his temple.' Was it Isaiah wrote that? or Micah? And I was looking to an unborn child, and you to a Rabbi from Nazareth, of all places!"

They sat quietly then, looking out at the ever-changing sea. Gradually Aryth became aware that the beach was becoming deserted. The few remaining fishermen, clutching their half-washed nets, looked about uncertainly, then dropped them in sodden masses on the sand. They called to their wives, who were already collecting their various children, and together they made their way up the beach, past the little hillock where Aryth had once been frightened by the crippled beggar. Beyond the hillock lay, as both women knew, an open meadow, grassy and green, often used for festal celebrations or for fiery orations—away from the city and its ever vigilant Roman police. From the city behind them others were approaching, in groups of two and three, all bending their steps toward that same little hillock and what lay beyond.

"Something must be happening," murmured Aryth, but Arusha seemed not to have noticed.

"Those prophecies," Arusha said slowly, hesitantly, "it has been so long—hundreds of years—I sometimes wonder. Are they still to be believed? Will they ever really come to pass? Or are they best forgotten, as God seems to have forgotten?"

Aryth shook her head determinedly. "No," she said. "He has not forgotten. How can you think so? Just a short time ago he sent his prophet to us, and in a very special way. He raised Amos and me from the dead. What greater proof do you need of God's love and faithfulness? He cannot forget!"

"But that prophet Jesus is dead too, like all the others!" protested Arusha, tears threatening again. "Can a dead man restore the kingdom? Or can he raise himself? How long must we wait before the real Christ comes?"

"Look!" cried Aryth, "Here come Father and Amos.

Something *is* happening!" And she sprang to her feet to greet them.

Amos ran to meet her. "It is Jesus!" he called out breathlessly. "His disciples say he is risen from the dead. He will meet them there in the meadow where he often taught. We must go to him!" He put his arm around her waist, and they ran together down the beach toward the intervening hillock.

But Arusha sat still under the acacia tree. "I do not believe it!" she said flatly.

"Arusha!" Jairus knelt beside her and gently took her hand. "You and I, of all people, cannot question his power over death. He raised Aryth and Amos, why not himself?"

She shook her head stubbornly. "I will not be deceived again!" she said. "I will wait here. You may all go and see what or who it is to see. It will be nothing! Come back for me when you are convinced!"

Jairus gave a short laugh of exasperation. "Arusha! This is not the time to let your usually overactive imagination fall flat! Come and see! It will do no harm, even if it is nothing!"

Reluctantly she allowed him to help her to her feet. They followed the others around the hillock into the green valley, and Arusha gasped.

"There must be hundreds of people here! But they do not know what they have come to see. They mill around like stupid sheep!"

Indeed, it was a restless, murmuring crowd, with no focal point and no sense of purpose. But there was an excitement there and an air of expectancy that affected even Arusha. They found Amos and Aryth on the edge of the crowd and joined them.

Suddenly Aryth cried out, and her voice seemed to carry over the whole restless throng.

"There he is! There where the ground rises and the rock thrusts out! He is raising his hands in blessing!" She sank to her knees, with Amos beside her. Then, like a field of grain bowing in the wind, those foremost began to kneel and the rest followed. It seemed to Arusha that in all that throng only she remained erect and unbelieving.

"Jairus!" she cried piteously.

"Arusha!" There was triumph in his voice. "He has conquered death. Don't you see? As no man has done before or ever will! He is Lord and God!" And he knelt beside his living daughter.

"But I cannot see him!" wailed Arusha.

Aryth murmured: "You must believe!" and reached for her mother's hand to draw her down. But Arusha desperately, hopelessly, resisted. This time she would allow herself no delusions. She would be totally honest. And she saw no one.

"Talitha cumi!"

She heard the words as clearly as she had once heard them beside her daughter's death bed, years ago. Yet she knew he had not said them, for here, among this throng of people, they would have made no sense. Or would they?

With an overwhelming surge of joy she realized that this time he was calling to *her*—calling her out of the death of her despair and unbelief into his life of faith and hope. And she saw him now, there where Aryth had pointed him out, and with the sudden surrender of faith she knelt beside Jairus in adoration of her Lord.

(This story is based on the Biblical accounts given in Mark 5:21-43; Luke 7:11-17; and 1 Corinthians 15:6.)

Joel of Tarsus

The square Hebrew characters were taking on a life of their own again, wriggling and squirming across the parchment like so many tiny black snakes. Desperately, Joel tried to focus his vision and steady his shaking hand as Rabbi Nathan approached. For a long moment the teacher stood over the paralyzed boy; then he lifted the thin sheet of papyrus from the table and held it up to the light, as if to examine it more closely.

"Hm-m. Did you bring in one of our doves and persuade it to step into your inkhorn and walk across the page?"

The sardonic voice penetrated thinly through the roaring mists in Joel's ears. But Reuben ben Aron's raucous laugh sent a surge of anger through him that cleared his brain sufficiently to allow movement. He dropped his shaking hand into his lap and waited.

Rabbi Nathan slapped the paper down on the table. "You are an intelligent boy. You come of a good family. How is it you cannot understand that not one dot or iota of the Holy Writings must be altered, even here in practice? Pharisee you may be someday; scribe, never!"

Joel sat silent, every muscle tensed to produce an outward appearance of calm. How could he explain his inability to capture and set down those small black characters when they began to move about of their own free will?

Rabbi Nathan must have sensed something of his agitation, for he spoke in a kindlier voice.

"Come, let me show you some excellent writing, done by a boy not many years older than you. He was not a great scholar, but a remarkable copyist." Joel pushed back his stool, supporting himself on the table as he rose. Beside him, Reuben ben Aron was cooing softly, and the smothered laughs about him were enough to steady his feet and straighten his back as he followed his teacher out into the corridor.

Nathan prattled on. "We gave him the task of recording the history and accomplishments of those who have studied here with us. It is an impressive list, beautifully scripted."

Through the haze which seemed perpetually to surround him these days, Joel realized that he had never before been allowed into the school's library, and he looked around with a faint interest. The walls were lined with clay jars, mostly of uniform size and shape, carefully labeled, and stacked upon shelves from floor to ceiling. Rabbi Nathan ran his hands lovingly along their glazed shoulders, then selected one slightly smaller than the rest. He withdrew from it the usual scroll, which he laid carefully on a low table in the center of the room. There he partially unrolled it.

"Rabbi!" a small voice spoke hesitantly from the doorway. Nathan turned impatiently. "There is disorder in the classroom, and Rabbi Gamaliel bids you come at once to quell it." The small messenger kept his eyes innocently wide and his mouth grave, but Joel bent his head to hide a smile. Strange how the least inclination to laugh always lifted the mists about him for a second.

"I shall come directly!" The boy disappeared, and Joel caught a muttered and decidedly annoyed "old man!" before Nathan turned to him again.

"Study it carefully. See how each character is well defined and properly spaced. There is no difficulty whatever in reading it. I shall return shortly!" The rabbi bustled away, but again a muttered "aged ancient!" brought a smile to Joel's face. No doubt old Gamaliel was a nuisance to the younger instructors. He had been a great scholar in his day—the grandson of the even greater Hillel, who had founded the school. But now, a decrepit, wraithlike old man, he daily wandered through the halls of the building, drifting in and out of classrooms at will, and occasionally asserting his authority in the most arbitrary and unpredictable ways.

Joel had little interest in the beautifully written scroll before him, but his vision had cleared a little, and he began to unroll it further, marveling that the letters now allowed themselves to be easily read. An inscription above one column caught his eye: "Saul of Tarsus."

With a slight quickening of interest, he bent closer over the scroll. His mother had spoken of Tarsus. She had lived there as a child and loved it because it was a beautiful city and one to be proud of as one's birthplace. Saul of Tarsus. Saul's parents had been . . . With a shock, Joel realized that Saul of Tarsus' parents bore the same names as Joel's own grandparents!

"Saul of Tarsus!" The quavering voice came from over Joel's shoulder. A bony finger reached out and tremblingly traced the name on the scroll before him. "Yes, yes indeed. He is your uncle, is he not? Your mother's brother? But perhaps you do not know. No, very likely you do not. He was a good student, one of the best that ever sat at my feet, though perhaps a bit overzealous. But a good student and scholar indeed, until . . . " he shook his gray beard in vague bewilderment. "Still, sometimes I wonder." He turned to drift back into the marble corridor, leaving his sentence unfinished.

For a few moments Joel stood there, trying desperately to concentrate. But the mists had drifted back into his vision as the dread had rolled back into his heart, and there was no use trying to read further. With shaking fingers he hastily rolled the scroll, set it back into the jar, and ran out the door, through the corridor, and into the open court. Circumventing the junior classroom where, by now, Rabbi Nathan had presumably restored order, he slowed his pace and cautiously approached the pillars that led to the vestibule at the main entrance. Only old Gamaliel was there, who nodded to him pleasantly, if vaguely, as he passed through.

It was always something of a shock to come out of the quiet of the synagog into the noise and bustle of a Jerusalem street, but this time Joel scarcely noticed. His thoughts were as chaotic as the bazaars around him. Who was this Saul of Tarsus, his uncle? In all his fourteen years he could not remember the name once having been mentioned at home. Not even in Tarsus—two years ago his mother and he had undertaken the long journey to visit his grandparents—not even there had he heard the name mentioned. But there had been a melancholy in that kindly home that even a twelve-year-old could sense. Was Saul to blame for that? Who was this Saul of Tarsus? What had he done that his name should be anathema even to his family? Was there more guilt to be atoned?

Directionless, confused, heedless of the noise around him, the dirt, the voices, the gathering dusk, Joel walked the crooked streets and alleys of the great city. Only when the increasingly steep inclines and stepped passageways indicated his nearness to the Temple area did he stop to catch his breath and look around him. The sun, long gone from the shadowy alley in which he stood, still lingered in golden splendor on the towering pinnacles of the Holy Place above and beyond the gleaming marble colonnades. He stood, thrilled as always, and a sudden clarity of brain and vision brought on the old familiar upsurge of delight in the beauty of the building and the joy of the Lord who had chosen to dwell there. "How lovely is thy dwelling place, O Lord of Hosts!" He had known the psalm almost since he had learned to talk, and loved it. The sense of peace it always brought hovered over him—but not for long. The black dread was upon him again, and he turned abruptly away.

It was not for him, the beauty of the Temple and the splendor of the Kingdom of God. He remembered Rabbi Daniel's solemn exhortations.

'The Kingdom of God," Rabbi Daniel loved to intone, placing the fingers of one hand precisely against those of the other, "will come at that point when, if even only for a moment, every member of God's chosen people stands in complete obedience to God's holy Law at precisely the same moment and without exception." Joel was convinced that he would always be the exception—the one who would delay the Kingdom and destroy the nation for whose perfection God had waited so long.

He had tried. How he had tried! But the gradual unfolding of the complexities of the Law during the two years he had spent at the school of Hillel had left him confused and despairing. The God of his childhood—the loving, caring God of the song of creation, of the patriarchs Abraham, Isaac, and Jacob, of the thrilling drama of the Exodus and Sinai, of the holy desert years, the conquering of Canaan, and the glories of the kingdoms of David and Solomon—that God was now as far away as his own happy boyhood. He felt suffocated under the restrictions and ceremonies, the sacrifices and prayers and tithes and atonements that grew more complex and rigid with every passing day.

For a while his home had been his sanctuary. The kindness of his father, the beauty and graciousness of his mother, the devotion of the servants, the wealth that could supply his every desire almost before it was expressed—all this, like a warm robe on a chilly night, had comforted and calmed him at the end of every school day. It was like living in two different worlds until, gradually, the world of Daniel, Nathan, and Gamaliel began to seep through the stout oak door and the stone walls that had sheltered him for so long. He began to realize that his father, though a Pharisee, paid little attention to those Pharisaic rites prescribed for the home, and his mother's gay laugh seemed entirely out of place in one whose chief responsibility lay in helping her son and her husband achieve perfection. They even seemed slightly amused at Joel's awkward attempts at ritual washings before meals.

Once his father had taken him aside and spoken to him earnestly. "Remember, Joel, God's love and his promises. They were given to Abraham hundreds of years before the Law was given to Moses. They are the heart and the soul of the Law and of our history. Do not let your teachers take the joy of God's promises from you with their rituals and ceremonies. You have known them since childhood. Hold to them tightly; you will need them!"

God's promises! Here in the shadow of the Temple he thought of God's promises, but they were not for him.

"God's promises," Rabbi Daniel loved to say, fingers precisely joined, "are for those who obey his Law."

Joel did not obey the Law. He could not. His father did not obey the Law. He did not seem to care. "The sins of the fathers shall be visited on the children"—as though he had not enough of his own for which to atone. For he found, to his mounting daily horror, that every new restriction, every more exact requirement aroused in him an anger and rebellion that threatened to destroy him. He hated Nathan; he hated Daniel; he hated the school; he HATED THE LAW!

He began to shiver, though the evening was warm. He felt utterly alone and helpless. There was no one to whom he could turn in his anxiety, not even God. He hated . . . But before he could think the unthinkable, he found himself running, the instincts of his childhood bearing him almost mechanically toward the only refuge that had not yet completely failed him. Dashing around the last corner into his own quiet street he ran full tilt into a tall young man in a yellow tunic. More stable than he, the man seized Joel's arm to keep him from falling. He was young and strong, with blond curls and laughing blue eyes, but his face showed his concern.

"Boy, are you hurt?"

"No, sir!" Joel righted himself quickly and drew back. But he could not resist an answering smile to the man's friendly warmth, and with the smile his heavy burden lifted slightly.

"I was waving farewell to my friend over there," went on the young man, "and not watching." But Joel had suddenly caught the meaning of the accent in the stranger's speech.

"You are a Gentile!" he cried. "You are a Greek and a heathen! You touched me! I do not allow a Gentile to touch me!"

The man straightened, and the warmth left his face. But it was sadness rather than anger that replaced it.

"Yes, of course!" he said. "May Christ forgive you!" and he went on his way.

Joel spat into the dust. Not only a Gentile, but a Christian! His dark eyes smoldered with anger. Forgive! It was the stranger who had need of forgiveness, not he! He was the son of a Pharisee, studying the Law, and—but the black wave of anxiety engulfed him once again. Hopelessly he watched the stranger disappear around the corner before he turned again toward home only to discover that the Greek's friend stood before his own door and was being admitted!

Paralyzed, Joel stood in the dusk, watching the light from old Gediah's torch stream through the open door upon the stranger. Of his own race, undoubtedly, and under a vow of some sort, for his dark hair was clipped short, and his prominent nose and reddish beard stood out in ungainly contrast. Nevertheless, he was the friend of a Greek and had no business in his father's house. Yet Gediah, with a broad, most unservantlike smile on his withered face, was admitting him. And Joel knew he would admit no one without his master's permission.

Joel waited a few minutes till he was sure the stranger had been ushered through the vestibule and into the court. Then he dashed to the door. Gediah was slow in answering his knock, and he banged fiercely upon the great oak planks. Once admitted, he tore off his sandals, wet his feet hastily in the bowl of water Gediah set before him, and ran off toward the court, leaving the frowning Gediah to wipe his grimy footprints from the polished marble.

They were there in the courtyard, the three of them. The torches had not yet been lit, but there was light enough so that he could see the gravity on the face of his father and the tremulous smile of his mother. The stranger was speaking. His whole body seemed to vibrate with the import of what he was saying, but Joel could not hear, for the little fountain splashed noisily between them. He crept along the gallery and into the shelter of a bank of flowers, hoping to hear but not to be seen.

"That is why I have wished for so long to see you," the

stranger was saying. "I remember you continually in my prayers. I want you, too, to come to know God's love, as I have come to know it, through his Son, Jesus Christ."

Jesus Christ! This man, too, was a Christian! Why didn't his father have him thrown out?

"We knew, of course, of your apostasy," said Joel's father, "and have thought of you as . . . as one might think of someone dead these many years."

"Ah!" The stranger lifted his face as though welcoming a great rush of fresh air in a stifling room. "But I *was* dead! Caught between the Law and my sin just as you are caught, if you would but admit it. Crushed between the two until my life was a living death, for I knew that sin earns only death. But in these days God has given us *life*—the free gift of a new life to be lived eternally—and has proved it by raising his Son to life again after his crucifixion. I have seen him—this Jesus, the Christ, who was crucified. I know of what I speak. He has made me a new man, free of guilt and of the fear of death, free of the curse of the Law. My sister, my brother, do not harden your hearts, but listen to me! Let me tell you."

Joel tiptoed quietly across the gallery and into his own room. He drew the heavy curtain across the door and threw himself face down upon his couch. He beat on the cushions with both fists until the great tide of fear and anger within him had been a little stilled.

This was Saul—Saul of Tarsus—his mother's brother and a Christian! His voice still sounded in the courtyard, a hazy murmur through the curtain. And his parents were listening to him!

Joel sat up and held his throbbing head in his hands. He had to think. There must be something he could do—some way of atoning for this defilement, but he did not know what it was. There had to be some sacrifice or vow. He would ask one of his teachers, perhaps even old Gamaliel. He would not dare tell them why he must know, but he would find out. He would do what the Law prescribed, first for his father and mother, then for himself.

But he had already so much for which to atone—his own rebellion, his hatred of the sacred Law. How could he take on the sins of his parents as well? Whatever he could do would be so pitiably inadequate against this great sin. The curse of the Law lay heavy on him, and he was frantic with fear and dread.

He threw himself down again and began to sob violently. He plumped a soft cushion over his head so no one could hear and cried until he had worn himself out. Then he lay exhausted, his mind throbbing dully to the rhythm that pounded in his brain: the curse of the Law, the curse of the Law, the curse of the Law.

"Free of the curse of the Law." Joel lifted his head. The phrase had changed. "*Free* of the curse of the Law?" Saul had said that. What did he mean?

Joel hurled his cushion into a corner and scrambled to his feet. He hesitated a moment at the curtain, then drew it aside. It was dark now, but the torches had been lit, and they flared fitfully in the evening breeze. His mother and father were seated on the bench beside the fountain, but Saul had pushed aside his stool and stood squarely upon his feet, as if impatient of anything that hindered his movements. Food and wine had been brought, but stood untouched on a small table.

"God *has* established his Kingdom among us, in the person of his Son, Jesus, the Christ. He lived among us; he healed the sick and made the blind see and the lame walk. He cleansed the lepers, cast out devils and raised the dead, as the prophets foretold, and at the last raised himself, also, after his crucifixion. I have seen him, and I know! *This* is the good news of the Kingdom: it is already here among us, and there is nothing we need do further but accept it by faith in him as Lord and Savior."

Quietly, anxious to hear every word, Joel crossed the gallery and stepped down into the court. His mother, without turning, held out her hand to him as he approached. He sat down on the flagstones at her feet and listened.

Saul went on more quietly. "He is living now, far above all heavens. But he has not left us alone. He has sent his Spirit to direct and guide us, to give us grace that we may be powerful in bringing others into his Kingdom. My brother, my sister, my nephew, will you not receive God's Holy Spirit? Let him enter your hearts and convince you of the truth of what I say!"

Far into the night they sat and listened while Saul spoke. Joel had never heard so wonderful a message.

The world seemed a different place to Joel the next morning. He had overslept and was late, but his heart was even lighter than his feet as he raced through the streets. Even his study of the Law seemed to have lost its power over him, for whenever the old fear and dread threatened to return, Saul's words came back to him: "Free of guilt and of the curse of the Law—in Jesus Christ!" And when it seemed to him that his relief and happiness must surely show in in his face, he bent his head diligently over the manuscript he was studying, and Rabbi Nathan commended him for his increased devotion!

It was hard to keep his mind on his lessons. It no longer seemed important—in fact, it was rather ridiculous—to learn that at the first washing of hands before meals he must hold his hands up to allow the water to run to his wrists, and at the second washing he must hold them down so that the water could drip off his fingertips. He kept thinking of what Saul had said about washing: "You are washed and set apart and made holy by baptism in the name of the Lord Jesus and by the Spirit of our God."

It was hard to keep his secret to himself. Though he had no real friends and companions among his fellow students, yet he wanted to stand up and shout: "This is not the way! The Kingdom of God does not come through the Law! Jesus is the Kingdom of God!" But he kept silent. He did not really know enough about it to explain it to others. And he knew only too well what would happen to a Christian here in the halls of Gamaliel. Hadn't he himself—it seemed years ago, but it was only yesterday—been horrified at the thought of coming into contact with a Christian? And here he was thinking like a Christian himself. What a strange power the words of Saul had, to change him like this! And how stupid and complicated all these washings and sacrifices and ceremonials seemed, when Jesus had made it so simple!

He raced home after school, hoping to find Saul there. But his mother said,"He is under a vow and is very likely in the Temple or with his Christian friends. He has much to do for the Lord. But we are happy he came to us when he did, are we not?" She lifted his chin in her gentle hands and looked searchingly into his face. Joel's answering smile reassured her. She kissed him and smiled in return, but her face was troubled. Joel knew how she felt. He too was happy and confused and troubled all at the same time. There was so much that was strange and different in this new revelation from God—this man, Jesus, who was God's Son and loved them. How he longed to talk once more with Saul!

Every afternoon thereafter Joel left school as soon as he dared and made straight for the Temple. It was not far, but the road was steep and narrow and crowded with pilgrims come to Jerusalem for the feast of Pentecost. And once in the Temple, Joel could not stay long, for his parents expected him home before dark. Indeed, Joel had no desire to be out in the streets after dark. He had heard too many tales of the roving bands of thieves and murderers who stalked the city after dark, in spite of the Roman guards. But he did want to find Saul.

Joel felt very small in the Temple, and he supposed that he always would. The great gilt-roofed colonnades with their tremendous marble pillars seemed as huge to him as they had in the days when he had trotted along beside his mother, clinging tightly to her hand lest he be swept away by the crowd of worshipers that eddied about the vast porches. He loved to stand at the base of one of the pillars, his hands touching the snowy coolness of the marble, his head thrown back so he could look up and up to the leaves and spirals of its richly ornamented top. There he would watch fleecy white clouds scudding across the deep blue sky in the open court and disappear above his head behind the polished roof of cedar that covered the colonnade.

But not these days. The magnificent pillars might have been ordinary gateposts for all the attention Joel paid to them. For a week he looked at faces—thousands of faces—realizing all the while how hopeless it was to try to find among them the one face he longed to see. When it was almost time to go, he would allow himself one last look at the Beautiful Gate. The great bronze doors were open, but never completely so, so that even from the outer court their burnished splendor could be seen and admired. Once Joel had been in the Temple early enough to see the gate opened. It had taken the combined strength of twenty men to push back the massive double doors.

There, one afternoon, Joel finally caught a glimpse of Saul. There were five men with him, four of them with their hair cut short like Saul's. The fifth was the Greek Joel had seen before. It startled him for a moment to see the Greek there, but they were well outside the marble balustrade beyond which no Gentile dared step. As Saul and the four Nazarites turned to mount the steps to the gate, the Greek lifted his hand in farewell and turned back to cross the court. But his way was almost immediately barred by a small group of men—not Jerusalem Jews, but wearing Asiatic dress—who advanced on him threateningly. The leader caught him roughly by the arm, but then, seeing Saul disappearing through the gate, released him and began to shout.

"Help! Men of Israel, help, help!" he cried. "This is that fellow Saul who attacks our Law and this holy place! Now he has brought Greeks into the Temple!"

"Greeks in the Temple! Saul has brought Greeks into the Temple!" The cry rose from all sides, doubled, redoubled, and doubled again, from the courts and from the porches. Joel caught a glimpse of the Greek, white-faced but free, dashing through the porches and toward the outer gate, from which he could reach the street. But in the court, like water released from a dam, the crowd surged forward and up the steps, led by the shouting Asians. Past the great gates they swarmed and into the sanctuary, while Joel stood frozen with horror, his hand to his mouth to stifle a scream.

Suddenly he felt a firm hand on his arm and knew at once that it was his father. He clutched at him desperately.

"Father!" he cried in terror. "Father, they will kill him!"

"Quiet!" warned his father. "We can do nothing. Stand quietly here, or they will turn on us."

He drew Joel into the shelter of a pillar, and from there they watched. The mob came pouring back out of the gate and among them they saw Saul, held between two powerful looking Temple police. There was blood on his face, and his clothing was torn. He was half dragged and half pushed toward the steps, and as he staggered and fell to his knees the great doors behind him, with thunderous noise, began to swing shut. The Levites wanted no murder in the Temple.

Above the uproar and confusion Joel heard a new sound, but before he realized what it was, the Romans were upon them. Holding their shields before them and beating about them with the flat of their swords, they drove in a wedge through the screaming mob and up the steps, where Saul's assailants seemed strangely to melt away. One of the centurions, a great giant of a man with a fiery red beard, lifted Saul as easily as if he were a child and set him gently upon his feet. The tribune, close beside them, gave an order, and chains were placed about Saul's wrists and one ankle. Then the tribune turned to the crowd upon the steps, apparently in an effort to find out who Saul was and what he had done. But the shouting and confusion only grew worse, and realizing the impossibility of making any sense out of the situation, the tribune signaled his soldiers and began to descend the steps.

The crowd, furious because Saul was about to be taken from them, refused to give way and pressed brazenly up and around the Romans. It was only by the most determined effort on the part of the surrounding soldiers that the tribune, followed by the centurion and Saul, made any progress at all.

To Joel and his father the Romans seemed a frighteningly small group compared to the milling, screaming mob about them. But they finally made their way out of the Temple enclosure and into the court of the adjoining fortress Antonia. Reaching the steps, the soldiers with a sudden thrust opened up a pathway. The red-bearded centurion seized Saul in his arms and ran up the steps, followed closely by the tribune. But there, in the doorway of safety, they paused. Saul was set upon his feet. There was some talk between him and the tribune, and then Saul turned to the mob. With the utmost confidence he raised his chained hand, signaling for silence, and, incredibly, the crowd quieted. Even at the very edge of the mob Joel and his father could hear that vibrant voice.

Now for the first time, Joel heard Saul's story—how he had, on the road to Damascus where he had planned to imprison certain Christians, been stopped by the appearance of Jesus himself in a blinding white light, and been converted. No wonder he could be so passionately sure of his message, even before a hostile crowd like this! No wonder he traveled far and wide, bringing this good news to Jew and Gentile alike! But when Saul mentioned his mission to the Gentiles, the fury of the mob broke out again. In a frenzy they began throwing dust into the air; screaming and shouting they tore off their robes and turbans, waving them over their heads and crying: "Kill him! Kill him!" Promptly the tribune ordered Saul into the fortress; the gate clanged shut, and the mob was left to howl fruitlessly outside.

Sick in body and heart, Joel and his father turned to go. As they stepped out into the darkening street, Joel drew a long, shuddering breath and his father laid his hand on his shoulder.

"At least he is safe now," he said.

"Safe with the Romans?" cried Joel incredulously.

"Safer than with his own people," said his father grimly, and in silence they walked down the steep and narrow cobblestone streets toward the quiet of their own home.

There were others at school who had seen Saul captured. Reuben ben Aron was telling the story with particular relish when Joel joined the group the next morning.

"What do you think will happen to him now?" one of the younger boys asked.

Reuben shrugged. "Scourge him first to discover what it's all about. Then . . . "

"Scourge him!" cried Joel. "They can't do that! He is a Roman citizen!"

Surprised, the whole group turned to Joel. Reuben's eyes narrowed.

"How do you know so much about Saul?" he demanded.

"I—I have heard it somewhere," stammered Joel.

"That is impossible!" Much to Joel's relief, everyone's attention turned back to Reuben. "He is a Pharisee and even went to this school. I've heard he has relatives in Jerusalem. How could he be a Roman citizen?"

"I heard the whole Sanhedrin is supposed to meet with him this morning," offered another boy.

"Yes. That is why Simon and Joshua and even old Gamaliel are not here. This time things will be different. Saul will be properly condemned and punished. See if I'm not right!"

Of the meeting with the Sanhedrin Joel heard later that evening. His father was even laughing a little about it.

"Saul made the Sanhedrin look like seventy inept fools," he said. "He knew he would not be fairly tried. The first thing Ananias did was order an attendant to strike him on the mouth. So he called out that he was a Pharisee and that the question at issue was the hope of the resurrection of the dead. So the old quarrel was on again, the Pharisees pulling one way and the Sadducees the other. Finally the Romans rushed Saul back into the fort, and they lost him again!"

"They will not easily forgive him that," said Joel's mother, white-faced.

"No. And what they will do next is not easy to guess. It will be bad for Saul, and they won't obey the Roman laws in this matter. When next they lay their hands on Saul, they will kill him."

Reuben ben Aron was full of mysterious hints the next day. He knew something, but it was a secret he would not tell. There had been a big meeting at his house early that morning, more than forty men, all Pharisees and all determined that Saul should not escape again.

"What fools!" said Joel. He hated to call attention to himself again, but he had to know. "If the Sanhedrin can do nothing, how can anyone else persuade the Romans to deliver him up?"

"The Sanhedrin is a bunch of doddering old priests and scribes that know nothing outside of their books," declared Reuben. "My father has said so. But these men, they are young and strong and . . . " his voice grew low and secret. "They have taken an oath! I heard it! They will not taste one bite of food until they have killed Saul! And to show they meant it they overturned all the tables in the room and spilled the food on the floor. I saw it all. I have a corner where I hide, and I see and hear many things!"

Joel laughed derisively, though his heart was pounding. "Impossible! They will starve! How can forty Jews seize a prisoner held by hundreds of Roman soldiers in a fort like Antonia?"

Reuben turned angrily on Joel. "You do not believe me, do you? Very well, you go to the Temple tomorrow and see for yourself. The Sanhedrin is going to ask to see Saul again, to ask him more exactly about his teaching. Before Saul ever reaches the council chamber, these forty will seize him and kill him! May they do the same to all Christians!" There was real hate in his eyes as he glared at Joel.

Joel did not wait till tomorrow. Scarcely were the boys dismissed before his flying feet brought him up the hill to the Temple court. There, walking more slowly so as not to attract attention, he made his way to the cloistered walks that led to Fort Antonia. He took a deep breath before entering the courtyard, but the lounging soldiers there only glanced at him curiously.

At the top of the steps he was stopped. "I wish to see Paul," he told the guard, being careful to use Saul's Greek name.

The guard called to someone inside. Joel was aware first of the great size of the man who issued from the shadowy interior; then he realized that this was the same red-bearded centurion who had rescued Saul. He felt a great relief: this man would surely help him.

"What do you want?" growled the centurion. "Don't you know that we Romans eat little Hebrew boys?"

Uncertainly, Joel looked up, but the centurion's blue eyes were twinkling under his frowning brows. "I—I wish to see Paul. There is something he must know. I must tell him." He did not know what else to say and stood there feeling very small and helpless.

The centurion laughed. "Take him to Paul," he said to one of the soldiers. "He does not look overly dangerous!"

The door to Saul's room was not locked, and Joel was relieved to see that he was no longer in chains. He looked alert and well, in spite of the great bruise on one side of his face. His eyes lit up at the sight of Joel.

"Grace and peace to you, my son!" he cried. "Come, sit here and tell me how I can help you!" He waved the guard away, as though he himself were the one in authority, and made room for Joel on the bench beside him. His robe was fresh and clean, and Joel realized that his Christian friends must have visited him to see to his needs.

"Indeed," Joel began, stammering. "I—I need no help. I came to help you. You are in danger."

"That, alas, is not unusual," answered Saul, with the flicker of a smile. "But what are my enemies plotting now, and how did you come to know of it?"

So Joel told him all that the careless Reuben ben Aron had revealed. Saul listened carefully, but did not seem greatly troubled.

"You have done well," he said. "I shall send you to the tribune, and you must tell him all you have told me. May our Lord Jesus bless you for your courage. You know that you are in danger if this is known?"

"Yes," said Joel. "I know. It does not matter."

"Then take care," said Saul, rising, "and God be with you!" Then, as Joel seemed to hesitate: "Are you sure there is no way in which I can help you? No service I can do for you?" The piercing eyes seemed to look right through Joel and into his heart.

"Yes, there is," said Joel, squaring his shoulders. "Tell me where I may learn more about Jesus."

"Now I thank God for you!" cried Saul, clapping his hands on Joel's shoulders. His face lit up with an inner glory, and the radiance of it brought a quick smile to Joel's face and a light to his heart. It seemed to him that all the inner anxieties and fears of the past months had been leading him to this moment, and he felt a great excitement.

"I shall tell you," said Saul, "and at the same time you may do me a service. Inquire on the street of the Cedars for Mnason of Cyprus. There you will find Trophimus, the Greek, whom I think you have seen before. Tell him that the Lord has not forsaken me. He stood by me in the night and promised me that I shall witness to him in Rome as I have in Jerusalem. Tell him to be cheerful and courageous and to stand fast in the Lord. Others who know of the Way will greet you there and will teach you the things of our Lord Jesus Christ. And now you must see the tribune. Guard!"

The guard had not been far off, and he appeared immediately.

"Bring the centurion to me!" commanded Saul. The guard disappeared down the corridor. In a few minutes the great red-bearded centurion stood straddle-legged in the doorway.

"What now?" he demanded. "Is it not enough that I strike off your chains and open your door to any half-grown young fool who says he *must* see you, that a Roman centurion in the service of the Emperor must leave his post for idle conversation with a Hebrew?"

"The Lord was wise indeed when he gave you so great a body to support so long a breath," commented Saul dryly. "Take this young man to Claudius Lysias. He has a thing of great importance to tell him."

The centurion cocked a bushy red eyebrow.

"To Claudius? This child? Hm-m. Well!" Then, as Saul's gaze continued steady and demanding, he shrugged his huge shoulders. "Very well! Come along, boy! To Claudius you shall go, no doubt to be thoroughly flogged for your arrogance!"

Uncertain, Joel hesitated. Saul gave him a little push, and Joel, seeing the reassuring smile on his uncle's face, took heart and hurried off after the rapidly disappearing centurion.

They walked through what seemed endless miles of corridor, and everywhere there were guards, watching with amusement the sight of the young boy trying to keep up with the giant strides of the centurion without losing his dignity. Finally they reached a small bare room with an inner door. The centurion growled to him to sit and catch his breath, lest he choke over his words to the tribune, and disappeared through the door.

The sound of talk and laughter from within the room did not reassure Joel. What would he say if he had to speak before all those Romans? And what would they do to him? He hoped Claudius would come out to him, but the centurion was at the door waving him inside.

Five or six centurions sat around the large, bare table, where there had apparently been a council meeting of some sort. Claudius turned in his chair as Joel hesitated in the doorway.

"Now here is a fine Hebrew!" cried one of the centurions. "This one surely we can scourge without hindrance!"

"Take care!" warned another. "These Hebrews are sly. Are you a Roman citizen, too, boy, like that Paul?"

Seeing the fright in Joel's eyes, Claudius pushed back his chair and rose quickly.

"Stop your jesting!" he commanded brusquely. "This boy shows a courage in coming here that would honor any Roman!" He took Joel by the arm and led him back into the small antechamber. "Now, what is it you must tell me?"

Carefully, Joel told his story. Claudius listened quietly, nodding his head in understanding.

"I am not greatly surprised," he said when Joel had finished. "Seldom have I seen such violent hate as his own people have shown toward this Paul. I have already considered measures for his safety. This means they must be carried out at once. After all, he is a Roman citizen. But you—you know that what you have done has put you in great danger from your own people?"

"I know," said Joel.

"Take care, then," said Claudius, "and tell no one that you have informed me of this. Antonius!" he called through the door. When the red-bearded centurion appeared, he said: "Take the boy safely to the street through the north gate, not the Temple court. Servius! Marcellus! Alert two hundred soldiers and seventy horsemen." Claudius' voice faded as he disappeared through the door. Antonius led Joel through more corridors, dark now and lit with flaring torches, till they reached a small door in the barracks' wall. He spoke to the guard, then stepped outside to look up and down the dark, deserted alley. Then he beckoned to Joel.

"Hurry now," he said, and laid a huge but kindly hand on his shoulder. "Get home to your mother before your priests discover who has betrayed them."

Joel hurried down the alley and around the corner to the street. But there he stopped. A slim moon was shedding a faint light over the cobblestones, but the frowning walls and looming tower of Antonia cut off his view of the Temple heights. In the deeply arched doorway of a shop just across from the fort he found a shadow where he could hide. He settled down there as comfortably as he could, glad that he had worn dark clothing, and waited.

There were not many people abroad at that hour. Occasionally a merchant, delayed at his trading, would hurry down the street on his way home to supper. The Roman patrol came by, with a great show of marching feet and clanking armor, while Joel shrank even farther back into his corner. Once a wedding party, with flaring torches and a great deal of laughter and singing and loud talking, shattered the quiet of the deserted street.

Through it all, Joel crouched in his corner. His legs began to ache, his tongue was dry, and he was ravenously hungry. But still he waited. Then, finally, came the sounds he was waiting for, and he rose to his feet expectantly.

The Romans were as quiet about it as they could be. The west gate of Antonia opened almost noiselessly. There were no flaring torches or ostentatious clanking of armor, only a steady shuffle of feet and low-voiced orders as the foot soldiers poured out of the gate and marched down the street. Then came horsemen, scores of them, and in their midst a light-robed figure—no Roman, even in the dark. Joel flattened himself into his corner, watching that robed figure till the great company had passed. Then he drew a sigh of relief and satisfaction, and went home.

Gediah and another servant met him a short distance from the house. Joel paid no attention to the old man's scoldings, but went at once to his mother's apartments. Here there were no scoldings, only his mother's relieved: "Joel, my son!" and his father's sterner: "What happened?" They sensed that this had been no childish escapade, and Joel was grateful.

Between bites of the food his mother set before him, Joel told his story fully, omitting only his request to learn more about Jesus.

"It is well," said his father. "You have done a man's work today. And there is likely to be trouble enough now for all of us. Do any of your schoolmates know you are Saul's nephew?"

"No," said Joel. "But Gamaliel knows."

"Ah, yes, Gamaliel. But he is old."

"He cannot go back there," interrupted his mother breathlessly. "They will know; surely they will know!"

"Father," Joel suddenly found it difficult to swallow and pushed back his food. "Father, I—I do not want to go back to Gamaliel's school. I want to be a Christian." Fearfully he glanced from one to the other of his parents, but his father did not seem angry, and his mother's eyes were shining. "Saul told me where to go—to Mnason of Cyprus on the street of the Cedars. The Greek will be there, and others who know of Jesus, and will tell me more of the Way."

Swiftly his mother came to his side and laid her light hand on his arm.

"I, too, would know more of this Jesus," she said in her clear, soft voice. "There has been a joy in my heart since Saul came to us that I had not known before. I must know more about Jesus."

Joel saw the grave concern in his father's eyes.

"Have you considered what this means?" he asked. "You will have no more friends in Jerusalem. Those who have been closest to you will despise you. There may even be danger when it is known that we, who are of Saul's family, are of one mind with him."

"All this I know," she answered steadily. "I, too, have despised Christians. May God forgive me! As to the danger," she looked down at her son, "Joel has not seen his grandparents for many years. They will welcome us in Tarsus. There are Christians, too, in Tarsus who will welcome us for Saul's sake."

Joel's eyes had not left his father's face. "Father," he said hesitantly, "you said 'we'?"

His father smiled. "Yes, Joel, we! I have known since Saul came to us that we could never again live as we had been living. Particularly would it be impossible for me to do business in Jerusalem if we followed in Saul's Way. And your mother's heart has always loved the gardens of Tarsus more than the palaces of Jerusalem. So let us go to Tarsus!"

But Joel's responsibilities were not yet quite fulfilled. "I have a message for Trophimus, the Greek," he said.

"Good!" said his father. He rose and clapped both hands on his son's shoulders. "Tomorrow morning early you and I will go to Mnason of Cyprus. Saul's escape will hardly be known till late in the day, and it will be several days before any suspicion might fall on us, for Reuben ben Aron will not be quick to confess his part in this affair. By then we shall be safe in Tarsus."

Joel felt as though the last loop of the huge knot within him had been tugged loose, and he was free. He smiled, gave a great sigh, and dropped back upon his stool.

"Mother," he said, "are there more of these figs? I'm starving!"

(This story is based on the Biblical account given in Acts 21:27 to 23:31.)